# SAVED BY VALOR

# SAVED BY VALOR

## RECLAIMING HONOR™ BOOK 7

JUSTIN SLOAN

MICHAEL ANDERLE

L M B P N

DISRUPTIVE IMAGINATION

SAVED BY VALOR TEAM

**JIT Beta Readers**

Alex Wilson
James Caplan
John Raisor
Joshua Ahles
Keith Verret
Kelly ODonnell
Kimberly Boyer
Micky Cocker
Paul Westman
Peter Manis

*If we missed anyone, please let us know!*

**Editor**

Lynne Stiegler

**Thank you to the following Special Consultants**

**Jeff Morris - US Army - Asst Professor Cyber-Warfare, Nuclear Munitions (Active)**
**W.W.D.E**

**From Justin**

*To Ugulay, Verona and Brendan Sloan*

**From Michael**

*To Family, Friends and*
*Those Who Love*
*To Read.*
*May We All Enjoy Grace*
*To Live The Life We Are*
*Called.*

# CHAPTER ONE

## Over the Atlantic

Flying in an airship back to Europe was definitely something Valerie never thought she would be doing, yet here she was on just such a ship, with some of her closest friends. Their mission: to bring a boy back to his family and see what they could do about a group of bandits who had been taking people from their homes and collaborating with the pirates of Toro.

This trip was infinitely more glorious than the journey that had brought her to New York. Every time she passed the cargo hold, she remembered hiding behind crates in that other ship with Sandra. That's where they had met Diego, the Werecat who had since stolen Sandra's heart. Soon they would be a family, and Sandra had threatened Valerie with death if she missed the baby's birth.

She planned on returning eventually, but it wasn't like she could rely on plans in this crazy world.

This time she occupied the captain's quarters; Captain Reems had insisted. Cammie and Royland had come too and were taking care of the boy, Kristof, but were on the other ship, captained by William.

Reems was still welcome in his own quarters, of course, and at the moment was sitting at the desk while Valerie etched a map into the bulkhead with her vampire claws. She could have used a blade, sure, but the exercise would have dulled the blade. With Michael's power surging through her, those claws were damn powerful.

"So you're suggesting we go north of the island?" the captain asked, pointing to the section she had just carved.

She took a step back, looking it over. She had created a map that showed the coast of America and Canada, including her best estimate of where New York, Prince Edward Island, and the Golden City were. She had also made little marks farther to the left to indicate Cleveland and Chicago, but didn't bother making sure the distance was to scale.

Then there was the ocean. She remembered sailing to America from France, and Reems had made a couple of journeys to Spain in his time, so they had jointly been able to piece that area together.

But everything north of France was conjecture. They knew there was land north of France, because they had both seen it on their travels. And she had met people who had made their way across the water, immigrants from England, Scotland, and Ireland, so she assumed those countries still existed. She wrote those three on the landmass, but had no idea how large they were, or exactly where.

They were currently over an island north of where she guessed the land once known as the United Kingdom had been. An initial push to the north to avoid a storm before heading east had brought them here. So far, the journey had taken them two days. Two days of sailing smoothly through the skies, two days of sailors telling stories and singing songs. There had even been a bit of dancing one evening.

She had been quite surprised at the pipes on the man named

William; that boy loved to sing. It was nice, because that wasn't something she heard much of. She certainly hadn't with the vampires of Old France, except for one night when she had gone out, watched a family, and wished she had that feeling with someone.

Then Sandra had come along and she suddenly *did* have a family, in a way.

"The island below us could be small or damn huge—I'm just not sure." She used the nail on her index finger to make a large "X" northeast of the island. "And to my understanding, our destination is somewhere over here, in a land once called Norway."

Someone knocked on the door.

"Enter," Valerie called.

Martha came in, her face pale. She had been a pirate of sorts, sailing and working in the open air. That exposure had given her skin a tanned, leathery quality, so pale on her was saying something.

"What the hell's going on out there that'd make you look like a ghost?" Valerie asked.

"Storm," Martha replied tersely, glancing at Reems.

Valerie turned to him now too. "Isn't it your job to steer us clear of storms?"

"My job is to get us to 'X' on that map." He stood, putting on his leather vest and a broad captain's hat. "The crew needs to warn me of storms before it's too late, so that I *can* get us through. I hope that's what is happening here?"

Martha gave him an apologetic shrug. "The crew isn't used to the skies this far east. I mean, really the best crews, the ones that normally went out this way, they were all with the prince, and likely died with the prince. We're sailing with the best we've got, but that ain't saying much."

"Spare me the excuses," Reems snapped, moving toward the door. He paused, looking over his shoulder. "I imagine we'll need all the help we can get, if it's bad enough to give Martha here the shakes."

Martha rolled her eyes, but sure enough, her hands were shaking. She quickly hid them behind her back.

"You weren't really much of a sailor, were you?" Valerie asked, grabbing her own hat and strapping on a sword just in case. For all she knew, they might find airships out there with pirates waiting to attack. Perhaps Europe had evolved pirates who were able to control storms for this purpose.

"Some of us on the island sailed, and some ran things on land," Martha replied, following them through the door and up the darkly-lit stairwell. "Since the land things side required less killing, guess which I chose?"

"Good for you, then," Valerie said. "Bad for us right now, though."

"If I could travel through time, I'd be sure to go kill a bunch of innocents to give us a better chance of survival right now."

"Hmm." Valerie paused on the top step, looking back with a smile. "Better to use it to go back a few seconds and refrain from snark, so I don't have to teach you a lesson."

Martha's eyes went wide.

"Joking," Valerie said with a laugh. "The day I start hurting people for speaking their mind is the day I'm no better than those I'm out here to put down."

"Good for me, because right now I'm feeling a lot of snark."

"Right now *I'm* feeling that you two need to shut up and follow me," Reems shouted, opening the doors that led to the deck.

Valerie nodded in mock submission and followed with a quick glance to Martha that said, *You made daddy upset.*

When she saw the storm, however, all humor vanished.

She might be a powerful vampire, able to heal from most wounds, walk in the sunlight, and even read minds—kind of. She could sense emotions, anyway, and right now a hell of a lot of fear was coming at her.

The fear made sense. A bit of it might even be originating from her. Hell, she imagined she would be able to swim for a long time if this ship went down or she was blown overboard, but the freezing waters would be damn uncomfortable.

And there was a chance that she might not make it. It wasn't like she had ever tested herself to that extent.

On deck, men and women were securing the barrels of food that had been brought out for the journey, stowing them below decks or securing what couldn't be moved. Most were heading to their sleeping quarters, but two sailors stood at the helm with their arms spread, hollering into the wind.

"Reems!" Valerie shouted.

Her voice must've carried over the harsh wind, because Reems stuck his head out. "Yes?"

"Make sure those idiots don't go overboard."

"You got it!" he yelled back, voice barely audible, and then ran over to check on his men.

Valerie supposed that something bad had to have happened sooner or later, considering what good luck they'd had so far.

The wind was picking up and soon strong gusts were bullying the airship, lightning breaking through the dark clouds that swirled about them. Raindrops were pounding the cheeks of anyone outside; it was clear the storm was upon them.

"Get us out of here!" Valerie shouted to Captain Reems at the entryway to the command center, then ran out to tell the others to get below deck.

The captain had just course-corrected and they were starting to steer clear of the storm when a loud ripping sound came from behind, followed by the ship's massive shudder. Valerie spun, looking up to see what had hit them.

*Oh, no.* In the chaos of controlling their own ship, they hadn't paid enough attention to where Captain William's ship was, with Cammie and the others aboard.

No confusion about where it was now, because its hull had just struck their balloon, rending a massive tear in it.

"ALL HANDS!" Captain Reems shouted, pointing to the hooks and ropes they had used for boarding other ships in their pirate days. "Abandon ship!"

CHAPTER TWO

**Over the Atlantic**

Cammie was below decks when the crash shook their airship. She and Royland had been talking with Kristof about his family for the last two days, asking questions about what they were like and what he remembered.

There was one story in particular that got to her. He told them about his older sister, and how she often took him to the waterfall to go swimming. One day she had played a horrible trick on him, jumping from the top and then quickly swimming to the spot behind the waterfall, where she hid.

When he couldn't find her, she had jumped out from behind the water to scare him. But seeing the tears welling up in his eyes, she had hugged him and didn't let go, hand patting his back as she told him she was sorry over and over. That was the day he always remembered after he had been taken from his home, and it was the reason he felt so strongly about returning. Sure, he missed his family and wanted to be with them.

But mostly he wanted to feel that hug again; to embrace his sister and be there for her like she had been there for him that day. He wanted to look her in the eye and tell her he would never leave her, ever again.

Cammie and Royland had held each other that night, after hearing the story. Just sat on the bed, arms around each other, heads leaning together, appreciating the moment.

"You ever have someone who loved you that much?" Cammie asked.

Royland laughed. "You love me way more than that."

"I mean, growing up?"

He frowned. "Growing up... Sometimes it feels like I've always been an adult."

"Yeah?" She laughed, then put her hand to her mouth to remind herself to be quiet, so as to not wake Kristof. "Then why do you act so childish sometimes?"

"First, I don't think that I do. Second, if I did, it would likely be to try and make you feel comfortable. You know, sinking to your level."

"*Pshh*, you don't want to come down to my level. It's deep down here. You'd drown for sure."

"Think a vampire can drown?"

She thought about it, then nodded. "Yes. I think you can heal from an awful lot, but you're not the immortal beast from stories, a devil walking or whatever. I think you'd die when oxygen stopped flowing to your brain and your brain stopped working."

He shrugged. "Makes sense to me...maybe."

"Maybe. But think about it, right? We've seen vampires die by decapitation, so I'd have to assume it has something to do with the brain. Otherwise, couldn't I just reattach the head and watch the healing powers go to town?"

"I'm not willing to be your experiment, so we'll just have to assume you're right. As always."

"Don't give me that shit just because I'm a woman." She shoved him. "I'm right an awful damn lot, but usually we're right about stuff together."

"Okay, now you're patronizing me," he countered with a chuckle.

They had talked for half the night, and then Cammie had curled up to sleep while Royland went upstairs to take the watch. Everything had been fairly uneventful until the next day, when the storm hit.

Chaos broke out and she ran below decks to tell Royland they were fine, but with the clouds coming in, he might soon have a chance to come on deck. It was quickly becoming dark as night, unless you counted the flashes of lightning.

She left him to care for Kristof and the dog, returning to the control room to check on William.

"Get us out of this mess!" she shouted, and he turned the wheel, face red with effort.

"It snuck up on us!" he countered. "I'm doing the best I can!"

She turned, eyes searching for ways she could help, when she noticed one of the female sailors slip on the rain-drenched deck, the wind blowing and, with the strong turn the airship was making, it looked like she was in danger of hitting the railing and going over.

Cammie rushed out, pushing with her Were muscles to leap farther through the air. She grabbed the woman around the waist and away from the rail, pulling them both to the deck and letting her claws come out and dig into the wood to hold them in place.

"Get below decks!" Cammie shouted, helping her to stand and running with her to the hatch. "EVERYONE GET BELOW! NOW!"

Thunder boomed, drowning out her final words, but the sailors got the message.

With the airship's deck being lashed by rain and the steep angle from the sharp turn, it was too dangerous for any of them to be out there. Cammie was about to join them when she noticed a flash of black that was too sleek to be cloud and too close to be the other ship. Too close, that is, unless they were about to collide.

Using her claws, she scrambled to the upper edge of the ship, the side angled toward the storm, and grabbed the railing, peering over.

Another flash of lighting, and sure enough, there was Valerie's airship below them.

"Pull up!" she shouted to William, but she knew there was no way he could've heard her.

As she watched in terror, the two ships moved closer together and, as William straightened out his ship to face away from the storm and make their getaway, their keel met the other ship's balloon. The force of it nearly threw Cammie overboard, but she dug her claws into the railing and hung on.

*"All hands on deck!"* Cammie shouted to William, who was peering out of the control room with a pale face. "We're going to need the sailors' help getting everyone aboard.

He didn't question her, just ran to the rear hatch to see it done, leaving her to stare down and wonder how the hell they were going to pull this off.

# CHAPTER THREE

**Over the Atlantic**

Valerie's ship had been struck and was, in all likelihood, about to be out of commission. But while the ship had grown on her, especially with the great logo her crew had carved for her on its side, the lives of the men and women sailing her were her responsibility.

She ran over to Captain Reems, chest pounding. "Where do you need me?"

"We don't have a chance with that ship above us like that. Don't suppose they have one of those comm devices or something?"

"You just brought me the one." She looked up, noting the angle of the balloon and the trajectory of their ship. She sure hoped she wasn't going to regret this. "Don't worry, I have an idea."

His eyes followed hers, then narrowed. "You can't possibly be serious?"

"It's our only chance, right?"

For a moment his lips twitched as if he wanted to argue, but finally he nodded. "Please don't mess this up."

"Believe me, I don't want to be at the bottom of the ocean any more than you do."

She got a running start, then leaped and grabbed one of the ropes that led to their quickly deflating balloon. She put all of her power into scampering up the side as fast as possible.

Gusts of wind blew and the ships shook, causing her to lose her footing more than once, but she held on tight with her right hand, refusing to give in. Whatever higher power was out there knew it wasn't her time, whether that was the gods, Michael, or simply herself. She shouted and pulled against the wind, clenching the rope with her other hand and then her legs. Rain pelted her as the storm started to catch them again.

"*Hurry!*" a voice shouted, carrying distantly in the wind.

Lightning flashed in the nearby clouds, lighting the dark sky, and for a split-second her mind went back to nights training with the Duke. Stormy nights, just like this, where he would have his closest few, his chosen, climbing buildings, scampering across electrical wires that had long ago been removed from use, and crawling through mud. In part, it had been to test them and train them for what was to come, but Valerie had always known that the larger part of his purpose was reminding them of their places beneath him.

Now she was at the top, in a sense; the most powerful being she knew besides Michael and Akio. Yet there she was, climbing some damn rope in the middle of a lightning storm over the Atlantic. She had to shake her head at the thought, wondering what sort of idiot got herself into such a predicament.

She finally reached the rain-drenched balloon at the top of their airship. It was losing air fast, though still maintaining its bearing, to a degree.

If it had been fully inflated, she wasn't sure this would have been possible. With all her power, she thrust herself up and out, losing connection completely, and in that moment she could imagine simply floating away, never to be seen again.

Then she connected, grabbing the balloon, nails digging into it. Her muscles bulged as she pulled herself up over the edge until she reached the point where she could run along the top. It caved in slightly with each bounding step, and each time she imagined the next one would simply pull her into its folds.

Not ten paces ahead she saw the other ship. She could even make out Cammie at its helm shouting orders, and then saw two sailors being lowered over the edge, preparing to cut her ship loose.

"HOLD!" Valerie shouted, her voice projecting over the storm. They looked up in shock, and one nearly had a heart attack. He slipped, the wind and rain doing their worst, and slid off toward the edge of the balloon.

Valerie threw herself forward, catching him with one hand as her free hand's nails dug into the balloon to keep them both from sliding off.

With a heave, she had him back on his feet and they joined the other sailor.

"Not yet," she told them when they were secure, then shinnied up one of the ropes they had left dangling over the side of their ship.

Cammie met her at the top, hand out to pull her up. Valerie took the hand, and was soon on the solid deck.

"What the hell do we do now?" Cammie demanded. "This is a complete shit-kerfuffle!"

"Shit storm," Valerie corrected her.

"Too easy, so no. But what's *not* easy is figuring out how to get us out of this mess."

"I got this," Valerie told her, darting toward the control room. "You just tell your men to cut us free on my mark."

Cammie gave her a skeptical look.

"Have I ever messed up something like this?" Valerie asked.

"There's always a first time."

"Not for me." Valerie reached the door and threw it open, then shouted back. "Get them ready!"

She waited to see that Cammie was conveying the order, then stepped in and closed the door behind her.

Judging by Captain William's wide, confused eyes, she must've been quite a sight. Wind-swept, drenched hair going in all directions, she imagined. If she let her eyes glow red, she would probably have looked like some storm god.

Her ears adjusted to the relative silence, and she stepped forward. "Time for some quality bonding time. And by that I mean, do exactly what the hell I say. Copy that?"

"Of course."

"Good." She gestured to the wheel. "Hard left when you feel us lurch, then I'm going to need you to bring us around so that we're nearly even with my ship."

His eyes lit up. "You mean to mount me!"

She frowned. "It's 'board' you. Yes, we mean to board you."

"Yes, same thing." He blushed, turning back to the wheel. She knew he'd just realized what he'd said, and had to chuckle despite the annoyance at how her clothes were clinging to her. A glance down, and she completely understood why his mind would have gone there.

Opening the door, she waved to Cammie. "NOW!" She nodded to William, and then it all happened in a blur. The ship jolted free, then practically nosedived, turning as she went. After a moment she leveled out.

Men and women shouted, then another jolt was felt as hooks met the side of the ship.

Valerie came back out on deck, watching as the ship, with her awesome carved skull and the new map she'd been working on in the captain's quarters, began to drop away.

"QUICKLY!" Eyes scanning the ship, she watched her men and women work their way over the rails. There was River, working to ensure that Martha was on a rope, but it wasn't looking good for him personally.

She turned, looking for a hook and rope. There wasn't time to act rationally, so she did the next best thing—she acted like a maniac desperate to save someone. She snatched up the rope and ran, swinging the hook as she did so, and jumped.

As she fell, she threw the hook so that it caught on the side of the ship, then held on tight as she swung down. With one arm, she scooped up River as her ship lurched onto its side.

Had someone not been on a rope at that point, they would have certainly fallen to their death.

Valerie jolted as the rope came to the end of its swing, but she held on tightly to both rope and boy, and then, as they started to swing back, she hefted him up.

"Hold on," she shouted, glad to see that he did. "Everyone up, before the next gust gets us!"

When they were all safely aboard she followed, falling to the deck after she topped the rail. She was keenly aware of the inch of water she was lying in, but she was already so soaked at that point that she didn't care.

"Will someone tell the captain to get us the fuck out of this storm?" she said, not bothering to raise her voice now. She knew they would be on it.

How the hell everyone had survived that, she had no clue. For what seemed like an eternity she just laid there, watching the rain. When it finally started to let up and rays of sunlight hit the airship's balloon, she sat up and scanned the deck.

The ship was damn full, half of them at work, half just trying to get out of the way.

They saw her sitting up, and started to cheer.

"Enough of that," she shouted, leaping up and pulling at her clothes, as if she could brush the water away. "You all did it."

"But we lost the ship," Reems admitted morosely.

She looked back at the storm in the distance. With her vampire sight, she was just able to see the shape of her ship where it had landed on the side of a hill, not far from the coastline.

For a long moment, nobody spoke. It was likely they were all waiting for someone, likely Valerie, to explode. This shouldn't have happened. One little storm, and they lost their shit.

Truthfully she wanted to go off on her captains, to start kicking stuff and swearing. That ship had started to grow on her. Instead, she just continued staring for a long moment, letting them all consider what had happened and process it in their own way. Getting angry at someone and trying to point fingers wasn't going to do any good now.

"Where is that, would you guess?" she asked, immediately followed by sighs or relief when the others realized she wasn't going to kick their asses.

A man stepped forward, the boy Kristof next to him. They spoke in a foreign language for a moment, then the man said, "Not a clue, but the boy remembers seeing that land on his way over."

Kristof nodded. "I distinctly remember that hill. I thought I'd never seen a hill so green in all my life."

"Wait, you speak the same language?" Valerie asked excitedly. "You're from the same area, then?"

The man nodded. "My family, it turns out, emigrated from near his town. Outcasts; left over from some dispute long ago. But I know his country, and spent some time there as a teen."

"Well, sir," she beamed at Captain William, "you might just be the hidden puzzle piece we've been looking for."

"And the islands?"

"My best guess? Judging by the size of the island, or what we saw anyway, I'd have to say the Faroe Islands. Not that I've ever been, but I've seen a map or two in my time."

"Remind me to go back and get my ship someday," Valerie commented, though she knew that was unlikely to happen. She really did like the carving, though, and the map, and would hate for those to fall into someone else's hands.

She turned back to the sailor and asked, "Do you think you could find this city, or at least the general vicinity?"

He nodded. "Not exactly, but the area? I can at least ask around, to get us there."

With a laugh, she turned to the crew. "Does anyone else not realize we are headed to Norway? Now that you know, does anyone have anything they can offer?" The crew laughed, and she held her hands up. "That's on me. It's taught me an important lesson about making sure to share my plans with everyone involved."

"We coulda told you that, boss," Reems said. "Like, I would've loved to have known about the plan to send one of our ships down like that. I would've advised you to send this one instead."

"Hardy-har-har." Valerie looked at him. "Tell you what, we find another awesome ship, she's yours."

"Deal."

Suddenly her eyes went wide and she ran to the rail, staring at her ship as if that alone would bring her back.

"What is it?" Cammie asked, stepping up next to her. "The comm device, it—"

"This one?" River asked, fishing it out of the pack at his side. "Why do you think I was late getting to the ropes?"

A smile spread across Valerie's face. "You angel! I knew I saved you for a reason."

He laughed. "You saved my life because you somehow knew I had this on me?"

"I'm an all-powerful, all-knowing vampire, don't you see that yet?"

"Hmm, must be that my simple human eyes are incapable of seeing such B.S."

Silence followed that remark, broken by Valerie's laughter. "Boy, I'm liking you more every day."

He smiled, then gave her the comm device and gestured to his wet clothes. "I'm going to check with William and see if there're dry clothes for everyone on board."

"Some of us'll have to go without a spare," one of the sailors interjected. "Tell him I said you can have mine."

"If he doesn't have the spares stowed away," River replied, then walked off to the control room.

"We need to get all of you dry," Valerie told Cammie, glancing around at the sailors. "I don't want anyone getting sick on this trip and ruining all the fun sightseeing."

"Sights?" Cammie laughed. "Ladies and gentlemen, on your left you have the lost airship of Valerie… Wait, how is it I don't know your last name?"

"Vampires kinda get rid of the whole last name thing. Just something we do."

"Huh."

"I guess it has to do with separating ourselves from our pasts." Valerie shrugged, turning to look toward their destination. "In a way, I get it. There's so much I'd like to forget. The path lies ahead and all that."

Cammie nodded, arms wrapped around herself for warmth. "Sure, that works. Makes sense, in a delusional sort of way."

"Excuse me?"

"Not meaning offense, but everything we do, every choice, comes from who we are and what we've been through. Hell, some would even argue we aren't really *making* the choice, that a combination of our past experiences triggers an automatic response."

Valerie pursed her lips, then shook her head. "Something's wrong with you."

"Oh, something's been wrong with me for a very long time." She shrugged. "But I'll take it, because it makes me who I am, and I happen to love that person."

"You are kinda great," Valerie replied with a wink.

"Hey, no winking at me anymore. Don't think I haven't heard about you and your carpet-munching ways."

"What the fuck?"

"Sailors talk." Cammie laughed. "Hey, it's nothing to be ashamed of. You don't think I've munched on a few carpets in my day? It was practically a carpet buffet back in the Golden City, though the buffet had much more to it than just that. That place was totally fucked up, honestly."

"I'm not a... I'm not repeating it. But I won't be reduced to some stupid label like that."

Cammie eyed her a moment. "You exclusive now?"

"What?"

"Meaning, if you didn't have the carpet, only..." She glanced around, her eyes stopping at one of the sailors standing watch, an arc rod hanging from his belt. "I'll word it this way. Would you rather lie around on a carpet, or be out there wielding an arc rod?"

"That's the weirdest metaphor I've ever heard." She positioned her hand as if attacking with an arc rod, moving to hit her opponent, and then frowned. "You've had your mind in the gutter so long, it's covered in shit."

"Fuck you," Cammie said with a laugh. "Just answer the question."

"You want to know if I'm dedicated one way or the other now?" Valerie rolled her eyes, turning away from Cammie.

Her feelings for Robin hadn't had time to subside yet, and it had never really been about the sexual side of their relationship. Sure she'd had those feelings, but that wasn't the whole of it. Thinking back to Jackson, it was kind of the same way. He had swept her off her feet, made her feel something, and not just with his arc rod.

Finally she sighed and turned back to her friend. "I wouldn't say I've made a choice, in that sense. It's about who I have feelings for. Maybe in *this* world, we don't have to make choices based on some physical aspect of the body?"

"Sure, sure… But which do you like more?"

"Oh, for the love of all that's holy, can we change the subject?" Valerie scoffed. "I mean, really! This is pretty damn typical Cammie right here, and I thought you'd changed."

"Me? Change?" Now it was Cammie's turn to scoff. "No, no, no. And no. I'm still as charged-up as ever. Just, now my energy's all flowing into one man."

"More than I need to hear, I'm sure."

Cammie frowned.

"But I'm happy for you," Valerie added. "I mean, really. Cammie settling down? That's something I never thought I'd live long enough to see, and since I'm some crazy powerful vampire now, that's saying a lot."

"Thanks," Cammie replied with a chuckle. "Surprised me as much as anyone, but at least I'm not about to have a baby anytime soon."

Valerie scratched her chin, considering that.

"What?" Cammie asked.

"It's just… Have you ever wondered if we're able? I mean, you're a Were, and we all know there are no problems there. But vampires?"

"*Now* we're getting into uncomfortable discussion topics." Cammie started to walk away. "Think I'll check on Royland. See about some combat practice with an arc rod."

"Wait, seriously?" Valerie blinked, trying to understand her friend. "You can talk all day about what's going on downstairs, but the minute I bring up children you freak out."

"Sorry, can't hear you over the wind!" Cammie smiled, then vanished below decks.

Valerie stood there staring after her for a moment, then noticed a sailor walking past.

"She could totally hear you," the man said.

"Thanks, I figured as much."

Valerie shook her head, unable to comprehend Cammie sometimes. She found herself talking with the sailor, hearing his story, then starting to tell hers. When she got to the part about her brother leaving her for dead outside Old Paris, she noticed half the sailors on the ship around her now, leaning on the rails or sitting cross-legged, listening like a bunch of school children.

"This isn't very exciting," she said, looking around at them. "I feel like the old woman with her stories."

"No, please tell us!" the sailor said, and the others nodded with wide eyes.

So she gave in, continuing to tell them about her journey west to Old Manhattan and how she had liberated it and stopped her brother from invading.

"It started as revenge, you know?" She looked around at them, quite sure not a one of them would be alive without having felt that at some point in their pirate communities. "I felt betrayed, alone...and, I'll admit, afraid. But that didn't last long, because I knew that the people of America needed me. They had a vampire army, led by the second most powerful vampire I knew at the time, heading their way to kill or enslave them. I had to get over there before him, to stop him and see justice done. Little did I know, justice would soon become my driving force in this life."

"So you intercepted him and put a stop to it?" the sailor asked.

"After a pirate attack on the way over, finding out that people were hunting vampire blood and putting a stop to a large portion of that, and making a few friends along the way, yes. I had a small army by the time my brother arrived, and with their help we took him out the moment he got there."

There were several mumbles of excitement about this. Valerie lost herself for a moment, thinking back to the moment Michael had arrived, interceding to level the playing field between her and her brother. Without Michael, the fight would have been one-sided, and she was pretty sure she would have died. He liked to keep his secrets, though, so she left that part out.

"One would think a city would implode after witnessing a battle between vampires like you're talking about," the sailor said, frowning. "I mean, hell, how'd you keep everyone from losing their minds?"

Valerie thought about that. "Most of the population wasn't around. It took place at night, and I remember lightning and rain, so they were probably inside. Most of the police and whatnot had suspicions, or there were the Enforcers. Many of them were actually part of the hunt for vampire blood."

This brought on new questions and Valerie relaxed, diving into the rest of her journey. By the time she told them of her final take-down of the corrupt and evil CEOs, the sun was setting and the sky was covered in streaks of purple and orange clouds. She left out key moments, such as meeting Robin and what followed with her. This crowd didn't need all the details, and the topic was certainly still too raw for Valerie to feel comfortable even hinting at.

She had excused herself and gone to the side of the ship to watch the sunset, leaving the others to discuss everything she had just told them. Some were skeptical about all of that being possible in such a short amount of time, but many of them were in awe.

A laugh snuck its way up and escaped. When had she gone from ultimate vampire warrior lady to storyteller extraordinaire? As long as it served to motivate them, she supposed it all worked out in the end.

"Land ho!" William shouted, stepping out of the control room and glaring at all of them for just sitting around. "You all want to get to work, or will we have naptime after story time?"

The sailors laughed at that and thanked Valerie for the tale before getting back to business.

"Story?" she asked no one in particular.

"Well, none of that really happened, right?" River asked. She hadn't noticed that he was still there, leaning against a barrel of food stores. "I mean, it's all pretty ridiculous."

"Is it?" She smiled, nodding to herself. "I guess you'll just have to wonder then."

He frowned, then nodded. "Okay, I'm done wondering. You were pretty badass on the island, but everything you just told us? No way. Not believing it."

"Hey, it happened. I did everything I just said."

"Keep telling yourself that." He winked and ran off, jumping out of her reach as she playfully tried to swat him.

"Get back to work!"

*Stupid kid*, she thought in amusement, and then turned to look out over the rail. They were sailing in smoothly, the land growing larger as they approached. Judging by the direction they had been traveling and assuming their guesses were right about what was where, this had to be it.

They had found Norway.

# CHAPTER FOUR

## Norwegian Coast

Sailing blindly across an unknown land wasn't first on anyone's list of suggested things to do. They all figured their best option was to sail over the land closest to the coast to see if they could find any cities.

At first it was amazing: the endless green, the fjords that rose like steep hills, intersected by beautiful lakes and rivers that shimmered like gold as they reflected the sunlight.

Sailors pointed out different colors of flowers and stared in awe at the land, and William started to sing again. The others listened for a moment, then some joined in. It was a melancholy song, but beautiful. One that brought Valerie to a time before all this conflict and responsibility. Images rushed through her mind of a day when she had been recently turned into a vampire and had felt lost, but had stumbled across an old tavern where men were singing. At the time, it had reminded her of her human side —maybe even helped her to not lose touch with that part of herself.

Of course, when her brother had slaughtered those men and smiled as he bragged about it later, she had spiraled into a state of confusion, but focusing on the part of the memory right before that and ignoring the horrible part brought a smile to her face. Ignoring the horrible parts had been the key to existing in her world before Sandra came along. Not anymore, though. She was done.

Cammie came and stood beside Valerie, smiling, hands in her coat pockets as she listened. She wore one of the pirate coats, a long black one with silver buttons, and it fit her nicely.

"How do they all know the words?" Valerie asked. "I mean, so well, and all at the same flow, or whatever you call it."

Cammie chuckled. "That's their way. It suits them, you know...the island."

"Sounds like they aren't the only ones island life suits." Valerie glanced at her, curious. "You talk like you might be considering never going back to New York."

"Guilty as charged," Cammie admitted. "Thing is, a big city like that just reminds me of everything I left behind from the old me. Out on the island, just sailing and keeping the peace, it's like I've finally discovered who I am, where I'm meant to be."

"And Royland has nothing to do with that?"

Cammie laughed. "Royland has a damn lot to do with that, and you know it. But I'll tell you, I doubt I'd feel any differently about it if he weren't in the picture. Much lonelier, yes, but no less fulfilled."

"Interesting," Valerie mumbled, totally lost in thoughts of Robin at that point.

Cammie just chuckled. "Okay, then."

"Sorry. I just need a bit of time to pull my head out of my ass."

"It's a big head, so that might take a while."

"Hey, shut your mouth about my head size." Valerie felt her head, pouting. It felt fine.

"I didn't mean literally," Cammie replied. "I meant your ego. I'm not the only one who has changed since we met."

Valerie nodded, smirking. "When you got it, flaunt it."

"I believe I will then," Cammie replied with a laugh, walking back to the hatch that led below. "And on that note, I think I'll go see how Royland is doing."

"Ah, rubbing it in my face, are you?"

"Yup."

Valerie shook her head, smiling. It was good to have Cammie back. It bothered her, though, that the woman fit in with her new surroundings so well. Not that she should feel bad about it, but she had kind of hoped that if she *did* go to space someday she would bring her closest friend and best fighters with her. Cammie certainly fit the bill in both regards.

The singing suddenly came to a stop and all were silent, simply staring overboard. Wondering what was going on, Valerie walked over and looked down. She understood.

It was their first sunken city, marked by underwater buildings whose upper stories protruded here and there. The coasts must've been hit pretty badly out here, she realized, wondering how much of where she had been so far, in New York and elsewhere, had once been occupied land that was now underwater.

The sight, combined with her talk with Cammie, got her thinking of New York. She lingered a moment, then retreated to the captain's quarters. Valerie pulled out the comm device and initiated a call to Sandra. When the other side picked up, a huge weight lifted from Valerie's chest.

"Still awake?" she asked.

"Val, you can call whenever you want. You have that privilege."

"This is crazy, right?" Valerie couldn't help but chuckle. "I mean, here I am across the ocean, talking with you."

"It wasn't that long ago the two of us crossed that same ocean."

"Yeah, I thought about that quite a lot on the way over." Valerie cocked her head, listening to the sailors play silly games. They must have passed the depressing scene below and one of them had been smart enough to find a way to lift their spirits. Good; she needed smart people under her. "I prefer not to think about the past. You know, because it's in the past and all."

"I hope you don't include me in that statement."

"You? Girl, you're my past, present, and now future, in a sense."

"And don't you forget it." Sandra laughed. "So...what's next for you?"

"We're looking for bandits out here, in part. Or, I guess, hoping we come across them as we try to find this boy's home."

"Remember what I said about being here for the baby's birth." Sandra's voice was stern.

"I don't come back in time, you kill me. Check." She paused, and then added, "We lost a ship."

"Excuse me? How does one simply *lose* a ship?"

"A massive storm will do it."

Sandra paused this time. "Oh. Damn. Wait, I see what you're doing here, no. You can die, lose another ship, whatever—I don't care. You *will* find a way to come back from the dead or swim across the ocean, whatever it takes."

"Noted." Valerie chuckled. "So you really mean it? No matter what?"

"No matter what."

The two talked some more about everything else in their lives, about Bronson and the children, and of course the café. Valerie was glad to hear it was thriving like always, but pulled back from the comm slightly at the mention of Jackson.

"He doesn't hold any hard feelings, you know," Sandra added, sensing the discomfort.

"I kinda left him stranded," Valerie argued. "*I'd* have hard feelings."

"Well, I guess that makes him better than you."

Valerie laughed. "Shut up, jerk."

"But no, really. He's been dating. And that girl you sent down, Clara?"

"Yeah?"

"He hired her for this charity thing he does."

Valerie just shook her head. "I don't think I'd recognize New York at this point."

"That's the goal." Sandra continued, talking about something to do with politics and trade, but Valerie stopped paying attention when she noticed something out of place on the horizon.

She squinted as she stepped over to the window, hand to the glass.

It was dark, but that had never affected her vision as a vampire. Whoever was out there had probably counted on it, because they were sailing in, fast, likely hoping for the element of surprise.

"Sandra, dear, I'm sorry," Valerie whispered, the immediacy of the moment clear. "Tell everyone I miss them."

"You okay?"

"Just unwanted company. Nothing I can't handle."

They said good-bye, then Valerie stowed the comm device and made for the deck. She found William and Reems at the door to the control room. William was clapping along as one of the sailors performed a dance that involved a lot of strange kicking.

At her signal, William and Reems followed her into the control room.

"I don't want to alarm everyone, but how much faster can this blimp go?"

William frowned with a shake of his head. "Not much faster, I'm afraid."

"I imagine there's a reason for that question," Reems said. "That's the part that makes me afraid."

"Without enhanced vision, you won't be able to see them yet," she told them, "but there are at least three airships headed our way."

"Hostile?" William asked.

"Could just be coming to check us out, but they're out in the dark, moving in fairly quickly." She frowned. "My guess is yes, they want us dead and looted."

"We can take 'em. We have you, and we have Cammie and Royland."

"If we can get to them, yes. But that would mean this ship had been shot down, in which case the rest of you could have been killed or badly injured. The other scenario is the three of us boarding the other ships and making a fight of it, but even then the chances of them not getting a critical strike against our ship are fairly low. They would have to get close enough for us to board, after all."

Reems ran a hand through his slick black hair, considering the situation. "We have to outrun them. It's dark, so we put out the lights, get the mountains on the other side of us so there's no silhouette, and we hide."

With a glance at William to confirm he had no arguments, Valerie nodded. "If it's doable, that sounds like our best bet. William on controls, Reems leading the sailors. I'll prepare Cammie and Royland in case there's trouble."

They agreed, and got to it.

Valerie found Royland and Cammie at the stern, teaching Kristof how to wield a knife. Possibly inappropriate in normal times, but considering the circumstances, Valerie found it fitting. She told them what was going on as she joined them, and the three of them stood at the back rail after Kristof had been sent back to their room.

"You don't need enhanced vision to see them now," Cammie noted.

"No," Valerie agreed. "They were much farther back before."

"You have a plan?"

Valerie told them what the captains were up to, casting her

eyes to the clouds, only to see that they were mere wisps across the moon. They wouldn't be much help—not for long, anyway.

"I imagine they'll set down at some point, when they've given up finding us, and then we'll strike."

Royland looked from the ships to her, his eyebrow raised. "Strike?"

"One ship for each of us," she told him. "When they're down, it shouldn't be a problem."

"You've grown…vicious," Cammie noted. "And I'm not sure I mean that in a good way. What if they're just defending their home?"

Valerie frowned and turned to Royland.

"Don't look at me." He held his hands up in surrender, but not to her. "I know better than to speak against my better half."

"Wow." Valerie just shook her head, unable to comprehend these two. "You've both gone soft. Fine, let them blow us out of the sky first, then we can decide if we want to hold hands and sing lullabies with them or rip their heads off."

"That's not what we're saying," Royland argued. "Just, maybe we should scout them. If they touch down, we get in there and see what they're about."

Valerie felt her brow furrow instinctively. "Deal. I'll get in there while you two stand by to defend the crew, if it comes to that. Once all parties are on the ground I don't want to leave them undefended, especially if we haven't decided our response level yet."

She could tell they didn't like the idea of her going out by herself, but if they didn't want to get their hands dirty, that was how it had to be.

A glance over the ship showed that all lights were out and the sailors were moving about their business, preparing hand weapons in case it came to that, and readying the ship's guns. It only had four cannons; no Gatling gun, as the Prince's ship had carried.

She breathed in the cool, clean air. It was nothing like the air in New York or anywhere else she had been, really. It was fresh; it filled her, made her more alert. Finding mountains to sail toward wasn't a problem, or at least large hills, which abounded around the fjords they were now passing over.

A glance down showed steel and rock and the ruins of other building materials sticking out of the water, and she wondered how many other cities had found themselves under water after the Collapse.

Moving through this terrain was going to be a challenge, but she looked forward to exploring new ground and finding out what these pursuers were after.

If they were the bandits who had taken Kristof from his home, which she certainly hoped they were, she looked forward to doling out justice.

# CHAPTER FIVE

**New York**

Sandra stared at the comm device in her hands, thinking how much she appreciated Garcia and TH for bringing this into her life. The thought of Valerie out there saving the world without any means of communication was terrifying. She still needed that crazy-ass vampire in her life, even if she couldn't be at her side.

There were others at *her* side, now. Garcia, Diego, Platea and Clara, even Bronson and his family. All of them together made her feel complete, like she belonged in this city. Like this world had finally accepted her.

What a long way she had come since her days as a slave to vampires back in France. Even if Valerie had treated her better than the rest, almost as an equal at times, she had always felt like an outsider, always known her true place.

But here? Here she was a leader, one of the people the city of New York looked up to. Not only had they seen her take down what they were referring to as a terrorist, but she had personally made the official proclamation that the city would once again carry the name New York. Technically it only referred to the area that had once been Manhattan; this New York was much smaller than the one from the days before the Great Collapse. Regardless, it was a great accomplishment for her, their soldiers, and the people of New York.

She had big plans for the city too, to be executed when pregnancy-brain wasn't getting in the way. There was so much she wanted to do, but her energy was at an all-time low. Being able to compare notes with another woman in her situation would have been great, but she didn't know any other pregnant women outside the crazy parts of town, and having conversations with anyone there was likely to end in a fight.

Instead she had taken to meeting with Platea over tea, an old tradition the woman had brought to the city. They were trying out the new shops that had popped up all over the city, what with trade improving as the city found stability after the piracy had been stopped. It was also, Garcia pointed out, good practice to not always be found at the same café. Change up the routine, so that if anyone did mean harm to Sandra or the others they couldn't spot a pattern.

"It's smart," Platea said, commenting on the strategy. "And thanks to him, we've found this place."

Sandra glanced around nervously, surprised this type of place even existed in New York. Where normally they would go to a restaurant for their tea— one older lady had even started a traditional tea house with shoji screen doors and all—this place just happened to have tea, but it mostly served drinks. The kicker was the shirtless men delivering the drinks.

"I'm not complaining," Sandra countered, "but I think Diego would."

Platea laughed. "Girl, this is for me, not you. He'd understand."

Sandra just nodded, not so sure. She'd never, not that she could remember anyway, really put Diego in a spot where she would find out if he got jealous or not.

The waiter came by to bring Platea another drink, and he

smiled when he caught Sandra's eyes darting across his perfect abs. She turned away with a blush.

"Fuck this." Sandra started to stand.

"No, come on!" Platea grabbed her arm. "Okay, just sit facing this way, away from them."

"Let the pregnant woman sit in the corner while you get lap dances?" Sandra shook her head. "Why am I here?"

"Honestly?" Platea bit her lip, then laughed. She motioned to the man, who apparently was still standing there, to Sandra's surprise. "Gill, right?"

The man nodded.

"Felix sent us. He wanted me to tell you he's feeling much better."

"Oh, thank God," Gill exclaimed.

"Wait." Sandra glanced around, only then realizing that most of the clientele were men. "Oh..."

"And Gill here is Felix' boyfriend," Platea informed her with a wink, trying to hold back laughter. "What kinda woman do you take me for?"

"I don't know *what* former pirates are into, honestly."

"I gotta get back to work," Gill told Platea. "But will you give Felix something for me?"

She nodded. He hesitated, then gave her a kiss on the cheek. "You can tell him to put that wherever he wants."

"I'm sure he'll say the lips," Platea replied with a laugh.

He nodded with a smile and moved on to the next table. The two guys there clearly looked uncomfortable, like they didn't belong, but couldn't hide that they were assessing the merchandise.

"This is the New York of the old days," Platea told her, motioning to their surroundings. "At least, that's how I hear it. Dance clubs, shows, and...this." Her eyes trailed a dark-skinned man as he walked by, and she made a soft growling sound.

Sandra laughed. "You're too much. Maybe we don't need to go back to *exactly* how New York used to be."

"Pick and choose what works for you, but don't stifle the other people's needs, as long as they don't impinge on society's safety."

"Yeah, I can buy that." Sandra glanced around once more, then nodded to the door. "Can we go now?"

Platea pursed her lips, then smiled wide.

"What?"

"Busted."

Sandra turned around, confused, and saw Diego and Garcia enter, both looking very uncomfortable.

"I vote we don't let Platea choose meet-up locations anymore," Diego commented as he joined them at the small table.

Garcia frowned, apparently confused about what was going on. After a moment his frown cleared, and he added, "Agreed."

"Ugh, you all are such prudes." Platea threw down some coins, enough for the tea and for a tip as well. "You going to get my back and tell them why we're here, Sandra?"

"Even if Felix asked you to pass on a message or whatever," Sandra replied, "I'm pretty sure you're really here for the man-candy."

She couldn't help but notice a disapproving glance from Garcia, and made a note to see what that was about later.

However, when the next waiter walked past, Garcia couldn't keep his eyes off Platea as she was checking out the shirtless guy and Sandra formed a good idea of what *was* going on there.

"Come on," Platea finally said, motioning them to a corner table where they could all sit and talk more privately. It was fairly dark in the bar, but that was likely part of the plan—to avoid being seen, to be cautious.

There hadn't been as much need for caution lately, but it was in times of calm that they all felt that caution was most needed. If it was quiet, then someone was probably planning something.

Maybe someday that would change, but they weren't delusional enough to believe that time was now.

"What do we know about this network of indies?" Garcia began. "That's our biggest issue. We make sure that's put down, and I'd say we're in the clear."

"Your army," Sandra asked. "Any more intel since…the incident?" She didn't want to mention what had happened to Felix around these two, as they were so close. And the boyfriend probably didn't need to overhear the details.

"It's like Clara said." Garcia nodded at Platea. "We put feelers out, grabbed a few of the nomads. Seems those wanderers aren't all as independent as we would've thought. Also, turns out there are a few communities that have been staying low on the radar. We still have to ensure they aren't going to cause trouble."

"So we're not talking about a quick kill?" Diego asked.

Garcia shook his head. "If it comes to it, yes. If we find out any of those bastards were associated with…the incident, then *hell* yes. But at first, I'd advise we think about this like a diplomatic mission."

He glanced at Diego, looked away, then looked back.

"I have dirt on my face?" Diego asked. "What?"

"You sure you're ready to get back out there?" Garcia looked genuinely concerned. "I mean, after… I don't want you getting trigger happy."

"You know me, and you know that isn't how I operate."

Garcia nodded. "Good enough for me. Sandra?"

"He wouldn't try to hold me back if the roles were reversed," she replied.

Diego leaned over and gave her a kiss, though she couldn't help but notice that he had done so right as one of the shirtless men walked by. Laughing, she asked, "Did you do that to show I was taken, or that you were?"

His smile gave nothing away as he asked, "Can't a man just kiss his gal?"

"Right…" She turned to Platea. "Theater. That was one of the things old New York was known for, and it looks like we have a professional actor right here in our midst."

"Laughing so hard right now," Diego declared sarcastically.

"I could honestly make it happen," Platea offered. "Up north I worked on outfits a bit. We got costumes, we got an actor."

"Not funny, ladies," Diego warned, but Garcia was staring off in thought.

"Actually, I wouldn't mind that," he stated. "What's the best way to get people's minds relaxed? Entertainment. We get a theater going, I'm willing."

"You'd get up there on stage and make a fool out of yourself?" Diego scoffed. "No way."

"I don't imagine I could play many roles other than myself, but I'd give it a try."

Sandra nodded, impressed. "Well, honey, now you have to. Can't let this outsider outdo you."

"Dammit." Diego leaned back and ordered a beer. He folded his arms on the table, looking at them. "What the hell! Could be fun. You get it set up, and when we get back, after a bit of R&R, we'll see what we can do."

"And if we need a big cat on set, we're golden!" Sandra couldn't help but laugh at her own joke, and the others chuckled to humor her.

"We'd better get to it then." Diego cut them off. "We could sit around laughing at my expense all day, but I think I'd rather be out there making a difference."

"Roger that," Garcia agreed. "Tomorrow morning, we get back out there and make it happen. I'll send someone ahead to tell 'em we're coming. Get an audience."

Good plan." Sandra nudged Diego. "And maybe we should be going soon. You know, give these two a moment to themselves."

Garcia blushed, but he wasn't the type to deny it, Sandra

knew. He shrugged. "Hell, I can flirt just as well with the two of you here. Problem is, I'm not much good at flirting in general."

Platea looked totally caught off-guard, but very flattered. "Well, since I'm the last to know about his... I can step up and do my part where flirting is concerned. But that's it, considering you have to be up bright and early."

"I find you interesting," Garcia replied. "Doesn't mean I'm ready to put out yet."

"You two, we're still right here."

Platea gave him a look, one he failed to interpret. Luckily Sandra was adept at understanding looks, so she pulled Diego up by the arm and said, "Dear, I'm feeling totally wiped. Help me home, will you?"

He glanced around. "But my beer!"

"Garcia here'll be more than happy to take that off your hands, isn't that right?"

Garcia was all smiles as he nodded.

"Oh, good God." Diego chuckled. "Gotcha. Right. Feeling wiped. Me too, actually."

Sandra rolled her eyes, but kissed him on the cheek as they left the two lovebirds behind. They exited into the hallway and made it into the elevator before Sandra pulled him in, loving that he hadn't gotten to the beer, since his breath was still minty clean and didn't make her nauseous. It seemed like almost every smell made her nauseous lately.

"What's this?" Diego asked, pulling back from the kiss for a moment. "Not that I'm complaining."

She held his hand as the elevator dinged. They had reached the bottom floor, so they stepped out.

"I get like this sometimes," she answered. "With Valerie, it was the same. It's like, sometimes I'm totally trusting, not worried and just knowing you'll come back. Other times, it's like I'm about to lose my mind."

"Well, don't go doing that. I need you right here when I return."

She rolled her eyes playfully. "I'll try not to."

"Good. Then I'll always try and return in one piece."

He kissed her hand and she nodded, then led him out of the building into the sunlit day.

# CHAPTER SIX

**Norwegian Fjords**

The sailors guarded key spots around the tiny valley they had set the ship down in. Reems had argued for higher ground, but William had made the good point that they wanted to be out of sight but still have the balloon ready to take to the skies on a moment's notice, if needed.

Cammie and Royland each led a fire-watch team, with the understanding that the three-person teams would set up a sleep schedule so that two were always awake and alert, one sleeping or resting.

Valerie, for her part, strapped on the largest sword she could find on the ship and then grabbed herself a rifle, which she slung across her back. She knew it would make an annoying clanking noise when she ran with it like that, but right now she was more concerned with having the proper weapons for a showdown.

She headed to the spot where Cammie and her team were on watch, then took a good look over the land. No other villages in sight, though the hills blocked the view in various locations.

Their pursuers didn't seem to care about giving away their

location. They had lit fires, and seemed to be having a party of sorts.

"Try to be safe," Cammie said, grabbing Valerie's hand and squeezing it.

Valerie went in for the real deal, wrapping her arms around Cammie and squeezing just a tad too hard.

"They won't know what hit them."

"Unless nothing hits them," Cammie noted, glancing back at her team. "Remember, you don't know who's on the other side."

"Seriously, did something happen to you while I was gone?" Valerie was about to walk off, when she froze and turned back. "Holy shit, it's the kid, huh?"

"What?"

"The kid, Kristof." Valerie shook her head, amazed. "He got to you, started making you see life in a whole new light, right?"

"Maybe I grew up a little," Cammie replied with a shrug, glancing at the other guards, who were watching them. "You all mind your own business."

"All right." Valerie adjusted the strap of the rifle across her chest, as it was digging into her boobs. "Just don't grow up *too* much. I miss the old Cammie."

Cammie's grin was the last thing Valerie saw before taking off into the night.

This terrain was different than any she had encountered before. It was more hilly and had much more vegetation, so running through it was harder. Being able to see in the dark was a definite bonus, especially when she came into an area of ground that nearly sank under her. She dove left, kicking off a rock wall and landing on the other side. She paused when she saw a wide and deep river before her, but identified a spot upstream where she could probably ford it.

More ruins jutted out of a swampy area farther north, so she avoided it, instead cutting due west, to the best of her ability, before she scaled a tall hill.

The terrain went on like this, but she picked up the pace, enhancing her run a bit with her vampire speed and adding extra boosts of power to jump over obstacles. Hopefully no one was watching; if they had been, they would likely have run screaming about a demon.

Finally she crested a hill and saw the fires below, so she slowed her pace and stuck to the shadows. She made for a clump of trees, where she knelt and listened.

Heavy breathing. Close.

She moved forward carefully, then saw the woman. She was standing guard, glancing about, but was apparently unable to see Valerie in the dark.

Valerie had just started sneaking by when another sound came. At first she was confused, then rolled her eyes—someone was tinkling. A glance confirmed that the woman had squatted.

Well, what did she expect, really? That these people could stand out here on guard all night and not relieve themselves? It wasn't like the woman was being rude. She didn't know Valerie was there, after all.

She kept going, trying to stifle the laugh that was threatening to burst out.

When she reached the edge of the tree line, she heard voices, and she stiffened at the first words uttered.

"Kill 'em all," a deep, heavily accented voice said. "We let anyone come onto our lands without our permission, next thing you know we're the immigration capital of Europe. Everyone will be up here."

"It's not about the land, you stupid fuck," a woman said. "It's about Flit and our promise. We live by his grace, like he told us. We bring him offerings, he leaves us to our worship."

"The hell with you and your worship—" *Smack!* Someone yelped, and a moment later the man's voice picked back up again. "What the fuck did you have to hit me for?"

"Pick up your guts and stuff 'em back in," she told him. "Don't get all soft on me because you're scared we didn't catch that damn ship. First light, we'll spot the bastards, and then they're ours."

Valerie frowned, inching closer. Something wasn't right here. It definitely sounded like someone was controlling them, or like they were beholden to someone who wanted sacrifices. That was rarely a good thing.

"Keep as many alive as you can, for now," the woman said. "The gods will go all teeth-gnashing crazy on us if they find out otherwise."

Another man spoke, this time in the language Valerie recognized from when she had heard Kristof and the sailor speaking. She figured it must be Norwegian.

"Don't speak to me in that pig-shit talk," the man said, and there was another smack, only this one sounded like metal on bone and was followed by a groan.

"What'd you go and do that for?" The woman shouted. "*Fuck!* You got blood on my new dress, you prick."

"Told them to keep it in the modern tongue," the man said. "Their language hurts my ears."

Valerie was done here. She had heard enough to know that these idiots got violent for no reason, and had bad intentions.

She was not going to let them reach her friends. However, asking a few questions in the meantime could only help. Turning back the way she had come, she made sure the woman had her clothes where they were supposed to be, then darted over, covered the woman's mouth as she picked her up and carried her out of hearing range. She slammed her down on the side of a grassy hill, hand still on her mouth, then leaned in close and *pushed* fear. Why show her the vampire eyes until it was necessary? This way the woman would be scared enough to talk without passing out in terror. At least she wasn't likely to piss herself, since she had just gone.

The woman's eyes went wide, pupils dilating.

"Here's the deal," Valerie hissed. "I want to know who the hell you are and what you plan on doing with us. Now, when I let go, you will do as I say or so help me, I will end you right now. Got it?"

The woman nodded as best she could with Valerie's hand over her mouth.

"Good. Talk."

Valerie slowly moved her hand away, *pushing* an extra tad of fear just in case.

"The gods of old, they're not far, half a day's journey north," the woman started, her voice shaky. "Kill me or not, you're dead either way."

"Gods?" Valerie laughed, this time letting the red glow show in her eyes. "I'm waiting to be scared... Huh, not happening. Weird."

The woman tried to scramble back, but being against a hill made it a futile effort.

"You... You're one of them?

Valerie shook her head. "There are no gods, at least not in the way you're thinking. I'm willing to bet my life on it."

The woman's eyes narrowed for a moment, then filled with tears. "Please..."

"Oh, fuck, come on." Valerie slammed her fist into the ground beside the woman's head. "No crying!"

"It's just... I don't want to be here, I didn't ask to be here. The gods...my family... I had no choice!"

Valerie growled, wishing it could be simpler than this. "Why can't you all just be bat-shit evil or finger-licking good?"

"Finger...?" The woman's tears stopped long enough for her to give Valerie a confused look.

"Never mind." Valerie considered, then, with a deep sigh, she stood and helped the guard up. "Here's what's going to happen. I'm more powerful than all your little friends back there put together. I'm likely going to tear your gods new assholes, because they sound like jerks. You're going to march back over to those trees with me and tell me who is being forced versus those who are in need of new assholes. Got it?"

The woman looked more confused than ever, but nodded after a moment.

"Let's get to it, then."

Just as Valerie had said, they walked over and, to her relief, the woman complied. They got closer this time, so she could see.

"There are lookouts there, there, and there," she said, pointing to several spots with trees or on hills. "I was supposed to spot anyone coming from your direction, so...yes, my mistake."

"Focus."

She nodded, then motioned to the fire closest to the airship. "Those are the ones you would say have no assholes."

Valerie considered correcting her, but found that silence was funnier here. "Wonderful. And the others?"

"They put the ones like me on the outer circle, so if there are attacks, we get hit first."

"Of course they did." Valerie considered, looking between the ships. "It's the same with all three?"

"It is."

"Okay, here's what you need to do if you want to live, and if you want anyone else who isn't evil to live." Valerie looked the woman in the eye. "Is that what you want?"

The woman nodded.

"Then we're of the same mind. Wonderful." Valerie tried a smile, hoping it would alleviate the woman's fear, but it seemed to just creep her out. "When I say go, I'm going to attack the inner circles. You tell your people not to fight, to retreat into the trees, and they won't be harmed. I've come here to put a stop to this sort of behavior—slavery, banditry, murdering innocents. Before I do this, can you confirm that is what I will be doing here?"

"It is," the woman replied, and Valerie felt an aura of warmth come from her. Truth.

"Then here it is: justice is calling. I'm going to answer the phone, are you?"

Again, confusion from the lady.

"Ugh. Just follow the plan." Valerie turned, drew her sword, and unslung her rifle. "*Go!*"

With a ferocious shout and a *push* of intense fear, Valerie burst from the trees. The effect was immediate panic. One of the men she was running toward stumbled backward into the fire, causing even more panic.

A moment later, the woman screamed something in Norwegian and half the closest group started running with her. Others picked up guns, some shooting at Valerie, some at those who were retreating.

Good thing for Valerie, because that made her feel much better about killing them.

She charged forward at vampire speed, spraying a handful of them with bullets before getting close enough to slash one in half. She spun on another and decapitated him. A woman charged her with a burning log, but Valerie swatted the log aside with her sword, lifted the rifle to the woman's head, and pulled the trigger.

More were coming, but the majority had fled.

Valerie charged, spraying more bullets and watching her enemies drop, then turned as a man landed in front of her, having just leaped over the side of one of the airships. He didn't seem to be in pain, which surprised her, and when he struck her, the blow actually *hurt*.

She took a step back, opened and closed her jaw, and then sniffed. Not a Were or vampire, but there was something there... An herbal scent. Bitter.

"What the hell are you?" she asked.

He grinned, lumbering forward. "Motherfucking Death."

"Well, Death, let me send you home." She darted around him,

bringing up her blade as she did so that it slashed his stomach open. "To Hell."

A glance down showed him his guts slithering out, but instead of displaying pain or fear, he simply put a hand over them to keep them in place as he turned on her.

"You've gotta be screwing with me," she said as he moved for another attack. He might be freakishly strong, and he apparently didn't feel pain, but he wasn't able to move at vampire speed. When Valerie struck again, she made sure the head went flying.

She was staring at the body for a moment, wondering what could have given him such strength, when she heard a noise.

One of the airships took off, then another.

She turned on that one, then noticed the last starting to lift as well.

"Dammit!" she shouted, slinging her rifle over her back as she ran to the closest one. She couldn't let them get away, not after what she had just done to them. Not after what they had just seen her do.

Her claws dug into wood as she grabbed the side of the ship. The gangplank disappeared above her, but the ship had cannon windows. She sheathed her sword, then used her other hand to claw her way over and thrust herself through the window.

A man fired his cannon, but she rolled aside and kicked it so that the shot hit the next man over. Unfortunately that man had a light, as he had been apparently preparing to light another cannon, and now the slowmatch he had been holding was dangerously close to the extra ammunition and other weapons.

Valerie debated her next move, eyes shifting between the growing fire and the remaining man.

"You're in trouble," she said, then winked and dove back out the window.

*KA-BOOM!*

The explosion sounded mere seconds after Valerie had hit the ground outside with a roll, and she immediately darted after the other ship. It was higher, but they had left behind two fighters to keep her away.

Both of them had shaved heads and a wild look in their eyes, and were accompanied by the same herb scent as the super-strong one.

Instead of bothering with them, she slid in to hammer-fist one in the crotch. When he didn't bend over from even that, she knew they were on some sort of drug; there was no question about it.

She recovered, then ran forward and scrambled up one of them, striking and clawing. He grabbed her in a bear-hug and she was amazed anew by his strength. She knew she was stronger, but didn't have time for an arm-wrestling match or a pissing contest, so she simply sank her teeth into him and drank his blood.

Instantly, he wobbled.

His momentary weakness was to her advantage. She broke his grip and pulled herself up, feet-to-chest, then held onto the back of his head and pushed, leaping into the air toward the departing ship.

When her claws sunk into this one, she felt something odd take over. The herbal scent was back, like white licorice—if there was such a thing—and suddenly she felt a brief surge of strength go through her body.

The drug, or whatever it was she felt, must've been giving those guys their strength. Damn, it wasn't bad, either.

She clawed her way up the side of the ship in half the time, then leaped over the side onto the deck just as her healing ability fought off the last of the drug.

Three men and two women turned on her, surprise evident on their faces. One stuffed a handful of strange leaves into his mouth while two others grasped metal bars and a third grabbed a crossbow.

Valerie deflected the first metal bar, then moved her head an inch to the left to let the crossbow's bolt fly past.

"You can all walk away from this," she offered, twirling her sword just for the show of it. "Just tell me you're nice people who only do nice things, and we're all good here."

The second metal bar guy said, "Suck on this," and tried to jam the metal bar into her throat.

"Be original, at least," she replied, slapping it aside and slamming her sword into his mouth, keeping the pressure on until it came out the other side. She *pushed* fear, and two of them ran, leaping over the side of the airship and likely to their deaths below, judging by how high the ship was now. They had just reached the top of the trees, and the glow of the flames below was long gone.

That only left two—the first to strike, and the man who had eaten the leaves. The one with the metal bar shouted something, and then they rushed together.

Like the men below, she could tell the one with the leaves would have incredible strength. Not that it helped him much when she stepped back and kicked the other man's knee out. He spun in response, and his bar caught the strong one across the face.

She sighed, sheathed her sword, unslung her rifle, and put two bullets into each of their heads. It was simply cleaner that way, though she did regret wasting the bullets.

When she turned to the control room, she found the door locked.

"Listen, I'm going to break down the door. Either open it and I go easy on you, or—"

A string of shots went off, shattering glass and door alike; it would've torn into her if she hadn't been so fast to react. As it was, a bullet skimmed her neck, leaving a line of blood. The cut would heal faster than she could stand up, but it still pissed her off.

In one beat of a heart she was in the room, tearing through two attackers, a man and woman, one dressed in black, one in white, which she thought would have been cute if not for the blood splattering across the outfits. Their own blood, no less.

The captain turned on her with a dagger, but she blocked the strike and tossed him aside. He landed on the wheel, causing the ship to turn, and then he attacked her again—except this time he dove to the right instead of striking, which actually surprised her. She turned, eyes narrowed in annoyance, and saw him pulling out a shotgun.

"No, thanks," she said. Quicker than he could react, she backhanded him so hard it spun him around and he fell to the ground, unconscious.

When she knelt to check his pulse, she smiled. "Good. When you wake, you can show me where this base of yours is."

She stood, then paused at a faint sound only her ears could pick up. Movement.

Glancing at her feet, she saw that the first man had an eye open and a hand in one of the drawers next to his control panel.

Expecting a weapon, she rolled her eyes, then stopped. *Oh, damn!* she thought as he revealed a grenade with the pin removed. She didn't need to ask what else was in those drawers to figure out there were likely more explosives. She needed to get the hell out of there.

She darted out of the control room and passed two more female bandits who had just appeared at the top of the stairs, ready for a fight.

"Gotta run," Valerie said, and darted past them to the edge of the ship. She looked for the nearest tree, and leaped.

*KA-BOOM!*

The rear of the ship behind her exploded as she slammed into the tree's branches. As she tumbled toward the ground, branch after branch hit her. She grabbed at each to stop her fall, and finally landed on the ground with a hard thud.

Flames lit the trees as bits of the ship fell on the surrounding area, and the balloon, now aflame as well, floated away without a ship to carry.

Valerie stood with a groan, turning to see the bodies of the two women not far off. Where the hell was she? She glanced around, trying to spot the fires where she had attacked the ships, but saw none.

After a crack of her neck and a quick breath to ignore the pain of her body putting itself back together, she ran to the nearest tree, jumped to the first branch, and quickly climbed its trunk.

Only, once at the top, she still had no idea where she was.

The ship had gotten turned around in the fight, and while it had been quick, she had no idea how far it had travelled.

This wasn't good.

She was lost.

# CHAPTER SEVEN

## The Badlands

Diego was happy to be outside the city, in that he wanted to get this over with as quickly as possible and ensure New York was safe before the baby came. He hated leaving Sandra to deal with the pregnancy by herself, but he couldn't expect the normal humans to go out and fight when Weres like him—who could heal and fight with enhanced abilities—sat at home with their wives.

He left with Garcia the first chance they got, after a quick stop to ensure Felix was doing as well as could be expected.

One of the vampires had earned himself the title of "Doctor" by figuring out how best to use the medical supplies recovered from the Bazaar—and now purchased from the enhanced trade—and he had started teaching others.

Their visit was brief, as the doctor insisted Felix not be woken, but as soon as they walked in to check on him, his eyes had fluttered open.

"You're going back out?" he asked.

"You bet your ass we are," Garcia replied. "Gonna get us some scalps for what they did to you."

"Dammit, I wish I could go. You sure this hole ain't healed yet, Doc?"

The doctor shook his head, glaring at Diego and Garcia.

"Yeah, yeah," Diego mumbled, then turned back to Felix. "Heal up soon, big man, or the war will be over."

"Gentlemen, he had a fucking hole blown through him." The doctor motioned to the door.

"Get some rest," Garcia commanded, patting Felix on the shoulder. "Maybe I'll bring one of 'em back for you to throw darts at or something."

Felix laughed, then groaned in pain, clutching the bandages over his wound. "I'd like that. Get me darts with little grenades on the tips. I miss the sound of explosions."

Diego had chuckled at that and said it was a deal, and then they were out and on their way.

Since Garcia had to take a whiz, they put the Pod down near a dead tree and the boys took turns trying to bring it back to life by watering the surrounding soil.

"I'll need another minute, gents," Garcia said, looking around for privacy but finding none. "Someone grab me something to wipe with."

"Ah, come on," Diego chided him, but ran back to the Pod to see what he could find.

It was a hotter day than usual, with flies buzzing around and heat waves on the horizon. The day had been harder still, knowing that Felix was back there wishing he could be with them, when really he should get a medal and be able to just relax for a year for going through what he had.

What was it with some people that made them feel like they had to be part of the action? Diego certainly understood the feeling—the need—even if he didn't understand the why.

Their first stop was one Clara had told them about, on the outskirts of what had once been New York City, not just Manhattan, which was what they called New York now.

According to her, the leader of the enclave was a woman who went by the name of Lady Woo, and she had a network of her relatives running the place. They ruled it like a militarized city-state, everyone forced to serve, but they were good at staying off the radar. Lady Woo was, according to Clara, fairly level-headed. That was why they had decided to try a diplomatic approach first.

Only problem was who to send as a diplomat. Sandra had volunteered, despite being pregnant. Diego was glad he didn't have to try to oppose that, because everyone else did. It just wasn't a safe enough world to have that make sense in any way.

Everyone agreed it would have to be a warrior, someone who had proven themselves to be diplomatic in the past, and that only left Wallace, the cop who had put Colonel Donnoly in charge.

"You don't want me out there," Wallace had argued, but Sandra and Garcia had both gotten behind the idea of sending him, so soon the others had gotten onboard as well.

"Who better?" Donnoly countered. "Me? I'd screw it all up with the wrong temptation. Garcia would likely snap their heads off with a dirty look, and Diego, well, he's too short to be taken seriously."

"Fuck you," Diego shot back with a smile.

Wallace had eventually agreed, and now walked at the front of the group in civilian clothes instead of the cross between soldiers' and policemen's uniforms he and the others had taken to wearing recently.

At least they had taken the Pod. Walking in this heat would've been unbearable.

"Almost done over there?" Diego called to Garcia, who was still squatting on the other side of the tree.

"Yeah, yeah," Garcia yelled back. "In a minute."

Diego turned back to the Pod. Clara sat patiently waiting for them, arms folded in her lap, her mother at her side. "You don't look much like pirates."

Platea glared. "That's because we're not."

"But you were."

"We were," Clara interjected. "Or, more like I was. Mom was just along for the ride, in a sense."

"So if it gets crazy out there?"

"Oh, we could take care of ourselves way before the whole pirate thing," Platea replied. "But then Clara here joined one of the worst pirate crews there was, and by 'worst' I mean best, but not high on the moral side of things."

Clara shifted uncomfortably, face red. "It wasn't one of my most clear-headed decisions."

"Made in haste just to spite me, I'd say."

Diego pursed his lips, wondering what he had walked into. These two probably shouldn't have been here, at least in his opinion, but they knew about this indie network, so they would likely serve as better go-betweens than Wallace. Having both options was a plus.

"That's going to be nice gift for the next Pod that stops by that tree," Garcia said, waving his hand in front of his nose as he approached.

"Tell me you at least covered it," Diego demanded with a scowl.

"I kicked sand on it, sure."

Diego just hung his head and sighed, then got back into the Pod. "Wake me up when we get there," He tried to ignore the look Garcia and Platea shared. They must've had a fun time chatting, because they'd been dressed this morning in the same clothes they had worn the day before, and had arrived together.

*They aren't even trying to hide it*, Diego thought with a smile.

When he opened his eyes Clara was staring at him, and he quickly looked away. That wasn't good.

"Wait! Oh, no," she held out a hand to get his attention, and it touched his leg. He jumped with a yelp. "Stop it! I wasn't like, checking you out or anything."

"Creepily watching me sleep?"

"Yeah, nothing like that. It's just, I haven't known many Weres who turned into cats."

He smiled, calming slightly. "Not exactly a cat, but yeah, okay."

Wallace glanced back at them. "Almost there. Keep it down."

"My apologies," Diego replied with a wave that became the middle finger as soon as the man had turned around.

He put it down quickly, realizing Wallace could probably see it in the mirrors. It wasn't that he disliked the man, necessarily. It was that he didn't like anyone telling him what to do, and he especially didn't like people who let prisoners get away. That's exactly what the guy had done though—Wallace had let his girl-friend, held prisoner at the time, walk.

"Whoa," Clara exclaimed, the first to see it.

Diego glanced over and nodded. "Yup, that'd be it, I'd bet."

Below them, hidden from view in a valley, was an old suburban neighborhood that had been transformed into a milita-rized zone. Around stacked cars was a fence that glistened at the top, likely from concertina wire, and past that several houses with a school at their center had been rebuilt to make them into a single structure with connecting passages.

"Doubt they get people flying in very often," Wallace commented, pointing to an area where several people had begun to gather near the old school building.

The pilot set the Pod down near the spot that they guessed was a gate, and they waited for the guard.

"We have reason to speak with Lady Woo," Wallace started, and Garcia cringed.

"I sent word," Garcia interrupted. "Please tell Lady Woo that Sergeant Garcia from New York is here."

"Not Chicago anymore?" Diego asked with a wink.

Garcia waved him off. "Shoot, after all we've been through? You're practically family now."

The guard frowned, confused, but then just nodded and went off to pass along the message.

"You guys have to act like that in front of them?" Clara asked. "I mean, I'd recommend putting more of a strong but amiable face forward."

"You're the expert?" Garcia asked with a scoff.

"In this place?" She shrugged. "Yeah, pretty much."

He assessed her, biting the inside of his cheek, then grunted. "Fine, no more shenanigans."

"That's all I ask," she replied.

Platea was smiling, trying not to laugh.

"What?" Diego asked.

"Count on Clara to put the big bad sergeant and the Were in their places." Platea was unable to hold back a laugh this time. "Typical."

"They're coming," Clara growled between clenched teeth. "Do you mind?"

"Right." Platea and the others put adopted stern expressions and waited as the gate screeched open.

"We got your message," the guard told them. "But Lady Woo isn't in the habit of inviting strangers in to see where we live."

"Our goal isn't to look for weaknesses," Wallace assured him, glancing around. "But if she doesn't feel comfortable in there, perhaps a ride in our Pod?"

The guard's eyebrow raised at that. "If you wanted her dead—"

"If we wanted her dead, we wouldn't have come here on a diplomatic mission," Garcia interrupted, "but fine. What do you recommend?"

Again the guard disappeared, apparently talking with someone, since their whispers carried in the hot wind. When he came back, he said, "She and a group of her people shall come to the closest building to this gate, nothing more."

"Wonderful." Diego took a step toward the gate, but the guard held up a hand.

"You must wait until her people are situated."

A few minutes wouldn't hurt anyone, Diego decided, so he simply nodded and stepped back, arms folded.

"And no guns," the guard added, before turning back and closing the gate.

Everyone stared at each other.

"I'm not going in there without a gun," Garcia said. "Look at this place! It's like an armory in there. They're guaranteed to be carrying."

"But doing what they say would be a good way to go about earning their trust," Platea advised.

"That, and showing you're weak," Clara added.

"Are these games really necessary?" Diego asked. "I mean, just shout at them to come out here and talk, and if they don't—"

"Don't even say it," Wallace advised. "You say what I think you're going to say, that makes you the bad guy. That makes you like the CEO, or Commander Strake. Lives are valuable, friend."

"You sound like a weird song person," Diego replied with a *humph.*

"A lyricist? I don't think so, and I really have no idea what you mean by that. I simply sound like someone who doesn't want to shoot first and ask questions later."

"Why do you know so much about so much all of a sudden?"

Wallace smiled. "What do you think I've been doing in the tower all day?"

"You mean HQ?" Diego shrugged. "Enjoying your time in the communal showers?"

Wallace chuckled. "No. Talking, listening, and learning. Our prisoners have much to say. I've mostly been hearing how *not* to act from them, but some of them opened up about their travels in this direction, about how people behave out here. Clara, tell me if I'm wrong, but hostility shown in this way

doesn't always mean they want to do us harm. It's more like...
to test us, right?"

Clara nodded, impressed. "Yes. They aren't bad people just
because they rub you wrong at first. They're probably trying to
figure out how much to trust us. After all, we did arrive in some
kind of technology they've not likely dealt with before."

Diego threw his hands into the air. "Fine, we leave our
weapons in the Pod. Locked."

"Deal," she replied. "Though I doubt they'd know how to open
the Pod even if it wasn't locked."

"It makes me feel safer to know it's locked.

"Makes me feel safer to walk in with a rocket launcher,"
Garcia noted, "but sure, I'll play along, I guess. Worst case
scenario, Diego here goes all catboy on them."

Diego glared, then stowed his weapons. "If shit hits the fan, I
want you all to pull back while I lead the fight, got it?"

The only one to refuse was Garcia, but Diego had figured on
that happening anyway. He knew it wasn't a battle he could win.

Once they had all stashed their weapons and locked up,
Wallace stood at the gate. "Done. We are unarmed."

Again the gate opened with a loud screech of metal, and the
guard motioned to them to follow. "Lady Woo awaits you
within."

He gestured for them to head for the closest building, as
promised, and took up the rear, his rifle at the ready, butt to his
shoulder.

"Don't get many visitors, huh?" Garcia asked. When he
received no response, he added, "You know, I figured that out
because of the whole gun and secluded thing."

This time the guard nodded toward the house and grunted.

"I'm not sure I like this guy," Garcia told Diego.

When they entered the building, they found themselves in a
hallway that led to two doors. The hallway had two more guards,
though at least they held bats and crowbars instead of rifles. This

made Diego curious—did they not *have* many guns, or were they simply low on ammunition?

Perhaps a trade network could be set up.

Their guard nodded to them and the hall guards stepped aside, pulling open the doors to reveal an assembly room with a chair on a raised platform at one end and more guards along the walls with weapons at the ready, though only a few guns.

It was Lady Woo, Diego presumed, who sat at the chair on the raised platform like a damn queen.

"You've gotta be shitting me," Garcia whispered, and Diego knew what he meant. If these people were really a bunch of psychos, this was a perfect trap.

He stepped forward, noting how the guards tensed. So, really not used to company. Also a bit nervous, which he took to mean they weren't sure how this would go.

Holding up his hands again to show he wasn't armed, he asked, "Lady Woo?"

The woman on the chair nodded. She must have been much younger than he had imagined, likely no older than her early twenties. How the hell did she get these people eating out of her hands? Her looks certainly weren't part of it. Despite her apparent youth, she had her hair pulled back tightly in a way that didn't compliment her pug nose or harsh eyes, and her skin was marked with scars and, on one side, a large burn mark. A warrior, then.

"We received your messenger," Lady Woo started, "so we granted you an audience, though I'm still not certain why."

"Why we've come?" Diego smiled. "We want to form a partnership."

"These people don't need more friends. They have enough of those."

"Ah, the network. Yes, we've heard."

Wallace cleared his throat, stepping up next to Diego. "We come from New York. Perhaps you've heard of it?"

She grimaced. "I hear you have some assassin who runs around dispatching her enemies in the night. If you've come here to scare us—"

"Not at all," Wallace interrupted. "And that's not what I meant. If you're referring to the person I think you are, I can assure you she's not a concern here. What I meant is our prosperity, and lately, our rule of law."

"Very much, lately," she countered, eyes narrowing further. "See, we Woos have long memories. Not even a year ago, Old Manhattan, as it was known then, was quite a different place. What's to say it won't change again in another year, or even six months?"

Wallace smiled, hands behind his back. "Quite simply, because of partnerships like the one we're here to discuss."

Diego had to give it to him—Lady Woo actually leaned back, considering his words. Wallace was speaking her language.

"Stability in Old, er, New York, does have its benefits. We've had our fair share of runaways from your neck of the woods, mind you. A system that put a stop to that would, as far as I'm concerned, help us out a great deal. Resources being scarce as they are…"

Catching on, Diego leaned forward and said, "Another area we might be able to help with."

Lady Woo looked intrigued by that, though Wallace shot him an angry glance before regaining his composure.

"Go on," Lady Woo encouraged.

Diego smiled and turned to Wallace, letting him take over so he didn't risk putting the other foot in his mouth. There was only one way to interpret that look, after all. Wallace had been intending to hold onto the information about trade and resources, to use it as a bargaining chip. Maybe he could still recover from Diego's little slip.

"The way we see it," Wallace said, slowly, considering his words, "there are several communities in the area. Correct?" He waited for her to nod. "If you helped us secure the rest, we'd be willing to send shipments your way. Maybe you start sending something back, or maybe it's as simple as setting up a larger network, like a Community Watch program. Each community sets up patrols, looking for problems, and puts a stop to trouble before it gets out of hand. Together, we bring peace to the American continent."

A glance at the guards showed this was going over well, at least with them. Lady Woo was leaning forward, hands clasped and fingers interlocked, index fingers extended to form a point under her chin as she considered the proposal.

Finally, she nodded.

"We can do our part, but there's a city not far north of here... They haven't traditionally played nice with us. You get them on board, and we have ourselves a deal."

Clara was the one to ask. "And the name of that city?"

"El Diablo," she replied with an amused grin. "Gotta ask yourself why, though, don't you?"

Diego shrugged. "I don't know. Seems like everybody wants to name themselves after the devil or whatever nowadays. I just assume it's because everything's fallen to shit."

The guard closest to Lady Woo tensed, but she held a hand up and he backed down, leaving Diego to wonder what the hell that was all about. He shrugged it off and turned to Wallace.

"Shall we leave immediately?"

Wallace nodded and was about to respond when Clara broke in.

"I've heard of that place. It's not exactly...a team player." Clara looked at her mom, worry heavy in her eyes.

"But you forget, we have Diego here," Platea said. "And I believe Lady Woo made it quite clear they *aren't* team players, which is exactly why we are needed."

Clara nodded, but the unease was still clearly present. Diego made a mental note to ask her about it later.

They had been hoping for a meal or some sort of grander reception, but as soon as they finished discussing the details and one of the guards gave them better directions to El Diablo, they were sent on their way.

"Not exactly the most hospitable of potential allies," Diego grumbled as he entered the Pod. He was the last one in, closing the door and sitting back as it rose off the ground. He turned to Clara and waited.

"Tell 'em," Platea advised. "Might as well get it out there."

Clara sighed, but nodded. "The pirates were actually planning to move against El Diablo. Probably would've happened soon if Valerie hadn't come along and disrupted everything. The deal was, they were part of the indie pact, but supposedly made some strong moves against their partners. Killed off a couple of key leaders. Maybe even gave Lady Woo that burn, if rumors are true."

Garcia frowned. "Then how does it make sense that she's so keen on seeing them join?"

"Good question." Wallace glanced over his shoulder at them. "If I was her, I'd have demanded that El Diablo burn, not be welcomed into the fold."

"Unless she's just the kind of woman we want on our team," Diego offered. "Not above moving on, forgiving, if it means being stronger. Better to have a group like El Diablo on your side than against you, perhaps?"

"But not if they betray their partners like the rumors say," Clara reminded them.

"True." Diego furrowed his brow in thought. "Something's fishy here. Can't wait to find out what it is."

"But we *are* going?" Garcia confirmed. "I mean, this El Diablo thing, it doesn't sound like good business."

"If it gets the rest of them on our side without bloodshed? Maybe it's just about setting this up right, putting people into the proper spots, maybe having some of our teams keep an eye on them."

"Oh, they'd love that." Clara laughed. "But hey, you are the ones who got New York rebuilt, so who am I to say?"

After that the ride was fairly uneventful, as was the scenery. Looking below them, they saw more brown, more heat waves, and more of the wasteland America had collapsed into. They didn't know what they were facing with this El Diablo place, but Diego was sure nothing could be good out in this hellhole.

# CHAPTER EIGHT

## Norwegian Fjords

Cammie had seen the movements by the fires of their supposed enemy and watched the two airships crash, though she wasn't sure how bad it had been for either of them, and the third moving off seemingly untouched. As the night wore on, Cammie started to wonder what the hell had happened to Valerie. Since the fires had died down, she was just barely able to make out the shape of the third airship, which was still aloft.

It moved north, and soon she saw its silhouette heading east against the sky. Odd—that wasn't the direction the airships had come from, so where was it going?

She wanted to get back to the others below and see if Valerie had checked in, but knew that wasn't what they had all agreed on. That, and as she stood there, her eyes began to close and her head nod.

"Why don't you get some rest?" one of the guards with her said. "It's your turn anyway."

While she did contemplate arguing, after a few seconds of trying to answer but nodding off instead, she agreed. Royland had been able to sleep most of the day, though he was lucky it was the other ship that had gone down. She couldn't imagine what he would have done if he had been forced to abandon ship. In fact, it was kind of careless to have brought him at all, but he had insisted. Now he was off on guard duty somewhere, completely rested, while she found an area behind the other guards and laid down, conking out within seconds of closing her eyes.

She woke with a jolt sometime in the early morning and turned her head to see one of the guards staring at her.

"What?"

He wrinkled up his face. "You're not going to like it."

"Valerie?"

He nodded.

"She didn't check in, huh?"

"No sign of her. William even came up from camp, asking. Nothing up here, nothing down there." The guard shrugged. "Nothing."

Cammie rubbed her eyes, trying to wake up. "This is so not good. So, so, *so* not good."

"They're packing up camp, said to get you."

She frowned. "So you let me sleep instead."

"No, I was whispering your name. You being a Were and all, I didn't want to risk getting my head bitten off."

"I wouldn't do that."

He nodded. "Good to know. Having not known many Weres, I'm not sure when to be cautious and when to treat you like everybody else. But I've woken my share of girls who nearly snapped my head off, and none of *them* were Weres, so…"

"Oh, shut up." She stood up, stretched, and glanced down toward where the airships had been. Sure enough, the third one was present now, but the other two still were gone. Smoke rose from trees far off to the northwest, barely visible at this distance. "I think we know which direction she went, at least."

The man turned, looking around and squinting in attempt to see.

"Right, it's too far for your eyes." She pointed. "There, just past those hills, there's smoke coming from the trees. A likely crash site, I'd say."

"The grayish blur?"

She nodded. "Keep up. We've got to get everyone moving."

They hustled back down to camp, and were just heading down the spine of the nearest hill when they came across three ragged men with horned helmets sneaking toward the camp.

Cammie glanced at the sailor with a raised eyebrow, then at the men. When she noticed the ax in one of their hands, an old pistol in another's, she decided that was a good enough to take them down.

"You wanted to see how a Were acts in the morning when she's pissed?" she whispered.

He looked at her with wide eyes and shook his head.

"Well, too bad." She stepped forward with a smirk, slowly removing the coat and then the blouse underneath. She didn't want to rip them, after all. "Oh, boys!"

When the three would-be attackers turned, their jaws dropped at the sight of the half-naked woman.

"I don't suppose you're here to steal, rape, and pillage?" She slipped out of her pants.

"This one's making it easy," one of the men muttered to the guy on his right, nudging him with his elbow.

"I'll take that as a yes."

The man laughed, hefting his ax onto his shoulder with one hand and starting to undo his zipper with his other. "Your friends will die, sure, but you might be just about to earn your ticket as my eternal love slave."

Cammie rolled her eyes at how lame these guys were. "I was so hoping you'd be a fucking ass-munch." At the look of anger that crossed the man's face, she smiled and leaped forward, transforming into her wolf form in the process.

The man yelped, stumbling back, but it was too late for him. She tore out his throat, then looked up at the other two.

One lifted his pistol to fire, but his friend had booked it so the pistolier turned and ran too, blindly shooting toward her over his shoulder.

She growled and pursued a few steps, then stopped, turning back to the sailor who was crouched on the ground. He had been holding his head as if that would protect against bullets if one happened to hit him.

As she transformed to human, he looked at her in awe.

"Ever wonder what a vampire does to a man he catches ogling his naked woman?" Cammie asked, holding a hand out for her clothes.

The sailor quickly snatched them up and gave them to her, turning away as she dressed. "You…weren't serious, right? About the vampire thing?"

"As long as I don't catch you eyeballing me like that again, you're safe."

"Th-thank you."

She finished buttoning her blouse, then threw on the jacket in time to see several of the sailors running over, led by William.

"We heard a scream," William said, "and gunshots."

Cammie gestured to the mangled corpse on the ground nearby. "There were two more, but they escaped. I imagine there's a larger group of them nearby, but we don't have time. I know which direction Valerie went."

William nodded, but told his men, "Station a team on the periphery until we're about to go airborne, just in case."

"Roger that," one of the men responded, then he and two others took off to gather more.

"I don't think they'll return," Cammie stated, wiping blood from her mouth.

"Me either," William replied, trying not to notice that she now had blood on her jacket sleeve, "but one can never be too cautious in a new land."

She nodded, giving him that.

When they reached the ship, she was pleased to see that they were nearly ready to set sail, and that Royland had Kristof tucked in on the ship, ready for some sleep.

"The boy was up half the night talking about how excited he will be to get home," Royland said, leaning against her and wrapping an arm around her waist. "I'll miss the little guy."

Cammie grunted, but he was right. "If it were up to me and no one else, we'd keep him."

Royland gave her an exasperated look, then nodded to Elroy, who was sleeping at the boy's feet. "Maybe he'll let us keep the dog."

"No, thanks. I don't need the competition."

He frowned. "Um, yuck?"

"Just saying. Aren't I bitch enough for you?"

"You're feisty," he argued. "Just enough for me to be perfectly happy."

She gave him a peck on the cheek. "Listen, I think I know which direction Valerie went, though I have no idea why she wouldn't have come back. Maybe she's off to take on this whole continent by herself."

"I wouldn't put it past her," he frowned, "but I'm pretty sure she would've told us first."

"Me too."

"If only we had one of those comm devices." He went to the window, just out of the way of the ray of light shooting through it, and stared at the fjords. "Assuming hers is still working. At least Sandra will know what's up. We could head back there when this is over, worst case scenario."

"*No!*" Cammie covered her mouth, glancing at Kristof, who

was still asleep. He didn't stir. Lowering her voice this time, she hissed, "I'm not leaving her here."

"I said worst case scenario."

"And I said no. That's not happening."

He nodded. "Then tell the team to get moving, because it looks like we have company."

"You've gotta be shitting me." She went to the window, anger flaring at the sight of specks moving across the hill—specks she knew had to be people heading for them.

"I hate this whole not-being-able-to-go-out-in-daylight business," Royland remarked.

"Got a sniper rifle somewhere aboard, I'd bet." Cammie nodded at the window. "Think you could manage without singeing your pretty skin?"

"The shots might wake the boy, but sure."

She laughed. "You really do have a soft spot in that old-ass heart of yours, don't you?"

"My heart's healthier than anyone else's here, I'll have you know. Old-ass, indeed."

"Only old-ass people say 'indeed' at the end of a sentence."

"So you're calling me a cradle robber, basically?" He rolled his eyes. "Just get out there and find me that sniper rifle, jail-bait."

"Jail...what?"

"A term from the old days, referring to the younger one in a situation with a couple where one's—"

"Not important. I get it."

He frowned but couldn't hide his smile, and she blew him a kiss as she ran off to find him a weapon. Soon they were ready, him at the window, her on deck shouting commands along with the two captains, though hers were focused on the disposition of those with guns.

The would-be attackers were now aware they had been spotted, and had taken cover behind a group of rocks.

One man stood, waving an overshirt in the air.

"Nobody shoot until I say so," Cammie ordered. "What the hell do you want?"

The man shouted back in Norwegian, so she turned, eyes searching for the sailor who was originally from Norway.

He rushed forward, out of breath, and leaned against the railing. "He asks who we are and what we did with their people."

"Tell him we didn't touch his people, and that we're looking for..." She glanced at Kristof. "What was the name of his city again?"

"Trondheim, and I'll tell them." He shouted back, conveying the message.

After a bit of back and forth, including yelling from both sides, the sailor pointed. "They claim it's half a day's ride that way."

"Half a day?" She considered this, then saw William approaching. "You heard?"

He nodded. "That could be where she went, thinking she'd meet up with us there after doing whatever else she needs to do."

"You," the Norwegian said in broken, heavily accented English. "Go. Home."

Cammie turned back to him, frowning. "We can't do that."

"Go. Home."

"Tell him we'll go home, but have business in Trondheim first."

The man listened, then shouted something before disappearing back behind the rocks to confer with his companions. Cammie gave a nod to William, asking him to be ready in case the man came back shooting.

However, a moment later the man stood and motioned someone else forward. It was a teenage girl, likely seventeen or eighteen, with short-cropped blonde hair.

"My name is Lillian," she said. "You may follow us."

"Follow you where?" Cammie asked.

The girl looked exasperated and discussed the issue with her companion, then said, "To Trondheim, of course."

This was unexpected. Cammie turned to William, then waved Reems over. She could see concern etched on each of their faces as well.

"What do you make of it?" Reems asked when he stood beside them.

"Could be a trap," she answered. "I don't like the idea of all of us leaving the one spot we know Valerie will come back to, but if we left some behind with these people knowing our location, it'd put the people we left behind at risk."

"It could be just you," William said, "but at this point you're our strongest day-walking fighter. It might not be smart to arrive in a new location without you."

"Agreed."

"We have no reason to trust them," Reems said, "but they also have no reason to trust us. Maybe we should tell them about the downed ship, see if they're upset or relieved once they see what it is, and then we'll know which side they're on."

"Not a bad idea." Cammie turned to the translator and nodded. "Pass that on."

While he did so, and the others discussed the possibility that they could be led to the wrong city, Cammie reminded them that it was Kristof's home. He would know immediately, and tell them if something was off.

She glanced over, watching the strangers as their man relayed the message. There was interest, maybe excitement, but no anger toward them. Mistrust, yes, but it didn't seem to her that these people were giving them any reason to treat them as enemies.

"Let them know there's a working ship there," she told the translator. "We'll help them get it off the ground." At the look she received from Reems, she added, "We have to show these people we're here to help, not cause trouble."

He nodded, though she could tell he didn't feel at ease with the idea.

"Send ten men with me, and tell them we'll fly in their ship. You all will follow."

"But you—"

"I can handle my own damn self," she interrupted. "If they try anything, I'll slaughter the lot and we'll have two ships. Nothing lost."

They all agreed, and soon she found herself heading off to join the locals, fingers crossed in the hope that they weren't stupid enough to try anything.

# CHAPTER NINE

**Norwegian Fjords**

Everything looked the same here, with the damn fjords creating hill after hill and more bodies of water to cross than Valerie was happy with. One or two hadn't been a problem, but this was getting absurd.

One thing was clear to her though, as she stared up at the blue sky with its fluffy clouds slowly floating toward her. She had gone the wrong way.

More than once she had attempted to course-correct, to make sure she was heading back inland, maybe south. She figured that was the direction she had come from, but nothing looked the same. It didn't help that they had set the airship down between some hills in a spot where nobody could see them—including her.

Now she felt as if she were walking aimlessly. It had been hours. `

At one point she came upon a stream, where she stopped to wash her hands. She found herself just wanting to sit, not because she was tired, necessarily; just bored with movement. For that moment, she just wanted everything to freeze around her and wait until she was ready.

A squirrel ran by, stopping to stare at her before skittering off. She was familiar with squirrels from her younger days, but couldn't remember the last time she'd seen one. Now that she thought about it and was paying attention, there were a couple birds chirping in the distance too.

This was a place of beauty in many ways that the American continent didn't have any longer. Even the way the sunlight danced across the grass as the leaves blew in the wind above was worth watching, and for a moment she was lost in its mesmerizing dance.

More than that, she found herself daydreaming, imagining herself and Robin running through these woods, throwing each other around on the grass. Maybe they'd be sparring, maybe a shoulder strap would come off…and maybe one thing would lead to another.

She smiled at the thought, even if it brought sadness. Not that she could blame Robin. They had set out to find her family, to rescue them, and they had succeeded. That was all the woman had wanted, so it shouldn't have come as any surprise at all that she had stayed with her family instead of heading off on a romp across the ocean to fight for justice.

Justice was Valerie's job. She needed to stop expecting others to drop everything to jump on board with her plans.

The word *woman* echoed in her head, as it related to Robin.

Woman… Valerie contemplated how the term fit Robin. At some point, she realized, it was how she had started thinking about her. Maybe it was because she was so deadly, so stoic, so mature? Or maybe it was the times in which they lived. while on some level she understood that Robin was young, on other levels it seemed like she was as much a woman as Valerie herself. Hell, in this world you were a woman the moment you had to start defending yourself against the crazies out there.

Odd how these thoughts hadn't really come up at the time, but now that she contemplated it, she wasn't sure how to analyze her feelings.

It was time to move on, figuratively and literally, so she stood and continued the journey.

More fields, more hills, more woods. But now she had something to think about, something to distract her.

Finally she spotted a shimmer in the distance, causing her heart to skip with excitement. She wasn't sure, even with her enhanced vision, but thought she saw a reflection of light. That was all—it could have been a lake, it could have been anything, but the way it came out of nowhere at an angle gave her reason to believe it might have been a window opening.

She darted forward, scrambling up the nearest hill, and stood at its peak to get a better view.

Aside from the gorgeous view of more fjords, rivers, and lakes with flooded ruins from what she guessed had been rising water levels after the Great Collapse, she didn't see much. The view took her breath away, and she marveled at the incoming fog when she turned to look west and saw the coast.

Judging by the direction she had just come, in relation to the ocean, and where the airship had sailed from, she could estimate where she was supposed to be. Unfortunately, she was nowhere near that spot.

She was fairly certain the place she had seen the reflection wasn't too far off, maybe somewhat north.

Funny how she could totally dominate in a fight, but felt like a lost child in a situation like this. But this wasn't the first time she had been outside her comfort zone, and she was determined to steel her emotions and kick ass here like she did on the battlefield. A punch to the nose there was the equivalent of finding high ground here to get a good view, a slice to the throat like ascertaining which direction she needed to go.

She decided she was going to slice this beast's neck and

devour the blood, metaphorically speaking. No more aimless wandering.

But first she had to be sure she was attacking the right enemy. One didn't strike randomly in a fight, but placed well-aimed strikes. Therefore she stared, focused on making the best decision she could with the information she had at hand.

Maybe she needed to go to the city. If the others had somehow figured out where they were, that would be their destination as well. In that case, heading there would be her best chance to meet back up with them.

She took off at a run, no longer feeling aimless once she put her mind to it. As much as she sometimes liked to think of herself as a lone wolf, this wandering business had taught her that only went so far.

Her legs carried her on and on, until she started wondering if there was a certain point where her legs would just stop working. If so, it certainly hadn't yet come. She was vaguely aware of a sense of exhaustion, but it really didn't affect her as it once had—especially now, when there was a chance of seeing her friends again so soon.

Valerie stumbled into a clearing of grass, one that led to a stone wall and an iron gate. She paused here, figuring it was best to approach as a friend rather than a foe.

A man appeared at the gate, hands on the bars. He spoke in Norwegian, and Valerie reminded herself to someday take advantage of the fact that she had a long time to live and try to learn languages other than French and the common tongue, English.

Holding her hands out to show she was unarmed, she said, "I'm not here for trouble. I'm lost, and looking for my friends."

The man leaned against the bars, staring at her. After a moment, he remarked, "This is an odd place to find oneself lost."

"You don't get many tourists then?"

"Tourists?" The man laughed. "Lady, someone comes here to be a tourist, they die."

"Is that a threat?"

He shook his head. "We don't kill them. It's the gods who get them."

"I keep hearing about these gods." She took a step closer and was glad to see that he didn't react. "Thing is, where I come from there *are* no gods. When you say it, do you mean the word in a literal sense?"

He considered her, then motioned her forward. When she was a foot from the gate, he lowered his voice and said, "You ask me to blaspheme, and the gods have ears."

"Ah," she whispered, "but it's only blasphemy if you say you don't believe they are gods at all."

He shrugged, leaning back now. "You need a room? Food?"

"Not particularly," she replied. "What I need is to find my friends, and I believe they are heading for Trondheim."

At this, the man's eyes narrowed. He stared at her, and she wondered what was going through his head. Energy flowed from him, giving her a chill and then a flash of something sharp.

"You're worried for me, yet…distrustful?"

He blinked, confused now, then unlocked the gate and motioned her in. "Quickly. It's best we don't speak out in the open."

This was an unexpected reaction. She ducked inside, following him along the walls and behind the buildings, where it was less likely anyone would notice them. One little girl chased a tiny pig and looked up at her with wide eyes, but other than that they went unnoticed.

He stopped at a hut with a curtain for a door, pulled the curtain aside, and motioned her in.

When she had ducked into the hut, he followed. It was dark, not that it bothered her. The only light was the dim glow through the thick curtain. The man, however, seemed restless—very nervous.

"You have something to tell me?" she asked.

He nodded. "If the others knew I was doing this, they might exile me. Maybe remove my head."

"Well, damn." She glanced around, found a bench apparently made from wood and animal hide, and decided to sit for the revelation. "Go on, then. No reason to wait and risk them coming around."

"Most are out," he told her. "Something about seeing outsiders, and then...the ships."

"I might have met your group," Valerie admitted.

"The ones *with* the ships, or without?" He looked very nervous at this.

"With. Yours are...without?"

He nodded. "They're afraid of the others, but not friendly. The ones with the airships, they took them from this group of bandits that has been gaining strength. Called themselves 'Vikings' and wore horns and all that shit like the old days. Some still do, but they've all been assimilated into this new group."

"Oh?" This was news indeed. "So this new group... They're not pirates? Or Vikings, I mean?"

He scoffed. "Are you asking if they steal and plunder? You're damned right they do. But they're worse than that; they're fanatics. And that's what I needed to tell you. That city you're looking for, Trondheim? They took that city about six months ago. Your friends go there, they're in for a world of pain."

Valerie ran her hand through her hair, processing this.

"What reason would you have to lie to me about this?" she asked. "That's the one thing I can't figure out. If you're telling the truth, I need to get to my friends faster than I thought, so I'm sitting here desperately hoping you're lying to me."

He laughed, but it lacked mirth. "I get the feeling you're not someone who should be lied to."

"That's right, but a woman can hope." She stood, not wanting to waste any more time. "How do I get there?"

He shook his head. "Is that really where you want to go?"

"What do you mean?"

"As I said, they own that city, but they have their homes elsewhere."

Realization hit her like a smack in the face. "And if I take them out at their homes, I don't have to worry about them in the city?"

He nodded, then turned his face up to the ceiling in thought. "Well, there'd still be the lookouts and the spies—those types in the city. But yes, if you had a force able to do that, your friends in the city would have much less to worry about."

Valerie smiled. "Trust me, I have such a force."

He gave her a skeptical look, then glanced around as if expecting to see an army surrounding them. "I don't see anyone."

"Trust me," she repeated, standing and nodding in thanks. "Where are they?"

"One more thing," he said, leading her back to the curtain. "This group, they came over from the land across the way. Iceland, it used to be called. Now I've heard they've started referring to it as 'the Fortress' on account of this new drug they've got. Gives them strength and helps them not feel pain, so nobody would want to try and attack that place. All because of some herb."

"I might have come across some of that too," she admitted.

"You...faced the drug?"

She nodded. She wasn't going to mention that she had sucked a man's blood who had just eaten the leaves and felt the power of the drug in his blood run through her.

"That, and I took down one or two of their ships."

The man's eyes went wide and he said something in Norwegian that she was pretty sure was a curse.

"Is that going to be a problem?" she asked.

"They'll be out for blood once they know that, and they'll come after us if they can't find you."

"Well, then, we'll just have to make sure there aren't any of them left," Valerie noted.

He sighed, shaking his head. "I wish you the best, and hope you have a damned army waiting out there. The gods might not be real, but they are *something*, and they're scary as hell."

"Where do I find these men, and…their gods?"

"The men will be in a city called Meldal." He held the curtain aside and pointed at a mountain. It didn't seem to be too far away. "There's where they live, just on the other side. While your friends," he pointed the opposite direction, "are that way, along the water. And then there are the gods. But the gods will find you."

"Good," she smiled, "because I'll be waiting."

"And your army?" he asked.

"It's just me, but that's all I'll need."

With that she ducked out of the door, scaled the wall, and leaped to the other side to be on her way. She didn't have any time to spare if she wanted to kill these sons of bitches fast enough to get back and find her friends.

# CHAPTER TEN

**El Diablo**

When the city of El Diablo finally came into view, Diego quickly understood where it had gotten its name. The city, if you could really call it that, was at the base of a small hill that had two dead trees on top—the trees looking like horns and some protruding rocks like the devil's face.

It also reminded Diego of the place where Felix had been wounded, and he found himself grinding his teeth as they approached.

"These guys try anything," he muttered as they set down the Pod a little way off, "and I swear to God I'll rip them all to pieces before letting them harm any of you. You can count on that."

"Good," Platea said, glancing at Clara. "But I think we should sit this one out."

"What?" Clara stared at her, then looked at the others for support.

Wallace shrugged with an apologetic grimace. "Sorry, but she's right. In this place we gotta watch out, you know, in case it gets dicey. You said so yourself."

"Using what someone said against them isn't nice."

"It's not really 'against them' if it's to potentially save their life."

"Sure, but you need us. We know—"

"We shared what we know," Platea interrupted. "We're staying in the Pod, and that's final!"

Diego had to agree with Wallace and Platea, and Garcia's dissenting grunt wasn't enough to change anyone's mind.

Their mission here wouldn't be as simple as the one in Lady Woo's city, though. As soon as they were within view of the city gates, the gates opened and a large group of humongous men and women walked out, each wearing a leather jackets or vest with a devil patch on the left shoulder.

"What the fuck do we have here, Arturo?" one of the largest of them said with a glance at the runt of the litter—who was still a foot taller than Diego. "You having a birthday party and forgot to tell me about the clowns you hired?"

Arturo laughed, showing teeth filed to points. *Wow*, Diego thought. He truly didn't know there were tools like this alive still.

A woman with striking red hair lifted a lead pipe onto one of her shoulders and spat, then looked Garcia up and down. "I like the Latin-looking one. You from down south, boy?"

Garcia took a look around, then nodded, running his tongue across his teeth as he assessed them. "Chicago, actually," he finally answered. "And I'll tell you what, I like you all. I mean it, really, right away you struck me as good people, the kind I'd like to call my friends. So what do you say, huh? Friends?"

Arturo laughed and a couple others joined in, but most of them just glared, understanding that he was mocking them.

"Get out of here before we throw you in the snake pit," the first speaker said. "Last chance."

"How 'bout this, Ugly?" Garcia took a step toward him, removing his camouflage jacket. Beneath it he had on a green tank top, displaying his taut muscles. "You and me. I win, you listen to what we wanna say. You win, we skedaddle."

Ugly smiled now, to his credit not even glancing at his friends for backup or trying to get out of it in any way. He simply stepped forward, took off his leather vest, and rotated his shoulders so that they cracked. In addition to being huge, he looked like a fighter—broad shoulders, a chunk of one ear missing, and a shaved head. That was probably why Garcia had singled him out.

"You sure about this?" Diego hissed to Garcia. If anything, *he* should probably be the one fighting, what with his extra Were speed and power. But Garcia was already committed, starting to move sideways and sizing up his opponent.

Wallace and Diego shared a look of hope mixed with worry, then stood there with their arms crossed.

The rest of Ugly's gang, however, were hooting and hollering, ready for the show.

A thud sounded, then another, and Diego stared in shock. It was the sound of Ugly's footsteps as he charged like a damned bull. The man's face was bright red, his meaty hands clenched into fists.

But Garcia was ready when Ugly tried to plow through him. The man had probably intended to tackle him to the ground, ending it fast, but Garcia moved into it, stepping slightly to the side to get around the man. He had left one leg out, sending Ugly sprawling into the dirt, and Garcia was on him in a blur of motion with a quick one-two punch to the face and back of the head, then a fast kick to the ribs before he leaped out of the way.

Ugly got up immediately, quicker than seemed natural considering his size, and started swinging like he was in a dark room surrounded by enemies. It was a mad flurry of meaty fists. When someone trained like Garcia had always done, they were prepared for most anything. A strike came, they knew how to block it and counter, or at least get out of the way. When it was chaos? Not so much.

One of those wild strikes caught Garcia in the chest, sending him stumbling back, and then order returned as Ugly charged.

This time he caught Garcia, lifted him into the air, and slammed him onto the ground on his back.

A loud *ooomph* came from Garcia as his wind left him, and then the first of Ugly's fists connected with a crack across Garcia's jaw.

Diego tensed, ready to jump in if needed, but he saw Ugly's compatriots waiting to do the same, a couple eyeing him. Not that they would have been able to stop him, but the glance and slight smile from Garcia were enough to keep him in place —for now.

Ugly's next strike came in the form of an elbow—but Garcia had wriggled and moved his head aside so that the elbow slammed into the hard ground beneath him instead. Ugly grunted and went for a chokehold, but Garcia was quicker and maneuvered out from under him and onto the man's back before anyone knew it was happening.

Now there was a move from the other side, because Garcia had delivered two good kidney shots and then put Ugly into a chokehold of his own. As the other big guy darted forward, baseball bat swinging, Garcia flipped Ugly onto his side, going with him so that the bat hit Ugly in the leg instead of taking off Garcia's head.

"Shit, I'm sorry, I—"

Ugly kicked at the man, breaking his knee as he wrested free from Garcia and rolled aside. Holding his throat, he croaked, "This is *my* fight!"

Again he was up and charging, but so was Garcia this time. The two met in the middle like ancient sumo wrestlers, shoving and punching, kicking and elbowing, until finally, with one especially loud crack of Garcia's knuckles connecting with the big man's jaw, Ugly wobbled, looked briefly like he was about to come back, and then collapsed.

A moment of stunned silence followed, broken only by a low groan from Ugly.

"Dammit all to hell," the redhead muttered, running forward to kneel at his side. "Micky! Micky, are you with me?"

The man apparently named Micky shook his head, eyes half-open, then managed to get out, "Yeah. Damn, Homeboy packs a punch."

"Pops ain't gonna be happy."

Micky, recovering, managed to push himself up on his elbows, turning to Garcia and then the others. "Deal's on. I'll handle Pops, as long as you tell this crazy son of a bitch to never hit me again."

Garcia laughed, then stepped forward. The redhead leaped up, lead pipe at the ready, but Garcia offered his hand to Micky. The man took it and stood, wrapping an arm around Garcia.

"This is what I'm talking about. This man right here." He turned to his group and held Garcia's hand in the air. The others seemed totally confused until Arturo yelled, *"Yeah!"* Then they cheered, everyone joining in.

*"Wooo!"* Micky turned his head and cracked his neck several times. "What a rush! That was a fight, for real. Shit, we oughta bring you out this way more often, see what you can teach these pansies."

Garcia laughed and nodded. "With the deal we're offering, maybe that could become a reality."

"Come on, then." Micky motioned to the New Yorkers to follow him. As he passed the redhead, he said, "Darla, calm the hell down and put that pipe away. We ain't barbarians."

She obliged, blushing, and followed with the rest. What ensued was the complete opposite of their incident with Lady Woo. These people treated Diego and the others like family, laughing the whole way and walking straight through their city without a care in the world about who saw what.

"Where the hell did you learn to fight like that, anyway?" Micky asked, still rubbing his jaw.

"A man out west of here," Garcia replied. "Goes by the Colonel."

"Shit! Terry Henry Walton—that Colonel?" Garcia nodded. "I've heard stories, that's all. But yeah, now it's making sense."

"You've heard stories?" Wallace asked, impressed. "Guess word is starting to spread, huh? Not the segmented city states we once were."

Micky nodded, leading them into a building that looked like a bar and boasted several whiskey bottles as decor. "You're right about that. The network around here's growing..." he shared a look with Arturo, "maybe too damn much."

"Fucking A." Arturo took a spot behind the bar and poured several glasses of whiskey, then handed them to their guests and Micky.

"The network?" Wallace started, but Garcia held up a hand, taking over. It was probably a smart move in this place, Diego decided, considering what they'd just been through.

"What can you tell us about Lady Woo and the others?" Garcia asked. "You see, we want to make this land peaceful again, but rumor is that you all and her lot aren't on very friendly terms."

Micky's eyebrows arched at that. "Rumors say that, huh?"

"Is it true?"

"Depends. You think sending two of your boys out to help someone and receiving their heads back in a box is friendly?"

A comment about giftwrapping and it depending on how they were wrapped popped into Diego's head, but he immediately dismissed it. *Not funny,* he told himself. *Not funny at all.*

"Damn," Wallace exclaimed, glancing at Garcia and Diego.

It was clear what he was thinking—who did he trust here? Judging by the reception at each place so far, Diego knew which way he leaned. As far as he was concerned, Lady Woo could go to hell. The only problem with that was, they needed the network and she seemed to be the key to it.

Well, perhaps they didn't *need* the network, but they wanted it. A system of protectorates forming a sort of Community Watch around the continent made a lot of sense, and would do a lot toward keeping the peace.

He ran his hands through his hair, and nodded Garcia's way. They had to pursue this relationship first, then figure out what to do about the whole thing. If these two communities couldn't work with each other, it would have to be dealt with. He had a feeling a lot more of these situations would be coming at them in the near future.

"Pops" finally arrived. He had to be in his seventies, judging by the harsh wrinkles on his leathery skin and his pure white hair. He stood tall, though, and proud.

Micky went over and whispered in his ear, then turned back and pointed at Garcia.

"This fucker right here."

Pops' expression didn't change. He looked Garcia up and down and flatly stated, "No way. This guy's not nearly big enough to take you."

Micky laughed. "Turns out size ain't everything, Pops."

"That's what she said," Pops muttered as if to himself, then burst into old-man laughter. The rest didn't get what was so funny, but smiled and nodded as if they had.

He joined them in drinking the whiskey, telling them stories about his time exploring the world, his attempts to partner with other cities and communities, and how it had so often led to heartache.

"But if you can pull it off, we're with you," he added, tossing back the last of his whiskey. "As for me, I'm an old man with a weak bladder, so I'm going to find a tree, then find somewhere to curl up and get some rest. Micky here will be my man until this is all over."

Micky nodded, gave Pops a hug, and saw him to the door.

When he turned back he put his hands on his hips, ample gut

sticking out and his grin proving he'd had his share of the whiskey.

"Let's do this, gentlemen." He strode forward, ground thumping, and shook each of their hands. "Consider yourselves now in league with the devil."

At this the room burst into laughter, though Diego only laughed along because he wanted to be a team player. *It really wasn't that original*, he thought, finishing his own whiskey as an excuse to stop laughing. The smile was at least genuine, because he felt they'd found one group they could trust.

When they finally started making their way back to the Pod, which was tucked at the edge of a ledge behind some tall rocks, Garcia and Wallace were staggering. Diego probably would have been too, but his rapid healing abilities had taken care of the alcohol pretty much as soon as they had left the gates.

They saw the Pod, doors closed, and something they hadn't expected—four large men in leather vests using bats and crowbars on the windows. The reinforced glass hadn't broken yet, but Diego could hear Clara and Platea screaming within.

"Hey," Diego yelled, breaking off from the other two in a run, "get the hell away from there!"

The four men turned on him and charged. He didn't want to give away that he was a Were, not out here, so he refrained from transforming. He prepared for a fight Instead, fists clenched.

As soon as the men were away from the Pod, its doors opened and Platea and Clara emerged, rifles in hand, and gunned down two of the attackers. The other two were too close to Diego to risk the shot, so he met them head on. He dodged the first strike, but a lead pipe hit him in the shoulder. He spun with it, turning in time to see the first attacker pulling back to connect with a jawbreaker.

Diego didn't like being betrayed. His nostrils flared and he swung, the punch connecting with the man's ribs with a loud crack. The thug stumbled back, coughing up blood, and fell, holding his side as he tried to breath. A punctured lung, no doubt.

The other man went for him just as Wallace and Garcia caught up. Diego wasn't letting them ruin his chance for revenge, though, so he quickly snatched up the lead pipe and blocked a strike, then thrust it so hard it punctured the man's skin as it sank into his belly.

"Damn." Garcia watched the man stumble back and fall.

Diego followed his enemy, took him by the hair, and asked, "What the fuck is this about?"

The man just laughed. "Pops decided he didn't like you after all."

That was all he needed to hear. A quick snap of the man's neck, and Diego went charging back toward El Diablo. He found Micky with an arm around the redhead, tongue in her ear.

Diego slammed Micky up against the wall, and it was clear Micky was surprised by his strength.

"What gives?" Micky asked, the redhead clenching her fists and looking around for the others. They couldn't move as fast as Diego, so they were nowhere to be found.

"Your goons tried to get us out there," Diego hissed between clenched teeth. "I'm figuring you have a death wish, because otherwise I don't understand why they hell you would attempt something so stupid."

Micky struggled to break free, but couldn't get out of Diego's grip. He looked at him with a wide, confused expression, then closed his eyes and breathed. "Lady Woo."

"What?"

When Micky opened his eyes again, they were calm but full of rage. "Let me ask you something. How are you sure it was our people?"

Diego opened his mouth to tell him it was the leather jackets, but then his mind reached back to the moment. His grip on the man loosened as he realized what had been missing.

"No devil patch, am I right?" Micky asked.

"Shit." Diego took a step back, considering this. "They wanted us to think it was you, then take you out—"

"So they wouldn't have to," the redhead finished, nodding. "Sounds like Woo."

Diego considered them for a moment, then nodded. "Damn, I'm...sorry. Don't suppose me bringing the best bottle of wine I can find next time I come out this way would make it up to you? Well, that, plus taking out Lady Woo, of course."

A wide smile erased the unease on Micky's face and he nodded. "That sounds like the perfect combination to me."

Diego nodded and took a step to go, but paused. "Just to be clear, if I somehow find out it wasn't her... If I was wrong, and get out there and find out those were your boys—"

"Come back here and do what you gotta do," Micky interrupted. "But I promise you it wasn't. We may be hard sons of bitches, but we got honor. We're loyal to the end."

Diego frowned. "Seems kinda contradictory to the whole devil motif, don't you think?"

Micky laughed, gesturing at his patch. "We wear it to say we ain't afraid. We know what's out there, and we say a big 'fuck you' to the devil, demons, whatever it is that tries to put fear in the hearts of men. Not us, no way."

Diego smiled. "I like that."

"Yeah?" Micky shared a considering look with the redhead, and she nodded. "Tell you what," he added. "Just to prove we got no hard feelings..."

He went back inside the bar and came out a moment later, holding a small leather vest with the devil patch over the heart.

"What's this?" Diego asked.

"It's yours, if you want it. Show the devil he don't mean nothing to you neither."

The redhead smiled and urged, "Go on!"

Diego stepped forward and accepted it, then tried it on.

"Damn, perfect fit!" He glanced at the two large people in front of him and pursed his lips in confusion.

"Yeah, I know what you're thinking." Micky sighed, closed his eyes, and when he looked up he had a tear in those large, fierce orbs. "Fits because it belonged to my boy. He was only fourteen. One of the two whose heads Lady Woo sent back. If you're going to take her out, I'd like... If it isn't asking too much, I'd like to be involved."

Diego ran his hand across the leather with new appreciation.

"Hell, you can lead the expedition. But we have to confront her about it first, get her side of the story, you know. As much as you're growing on me, we have to be sure we know the truth."

"I wouldn't expect any less," the man agreed. "I'll gather my troops and get ready. You start the fight, then give us a signal and we'll come charging."

Diego nodded. "Thanks again for the vest."

"We'll see you soon," Micky replied, and held out his arms.

"You... He's serious about this?" Diego asked, glancing between Micky and Darla.

"Micky's a hugger," the redhead replied with a laugh. "Best get in there before he rescinds the offer."

Micky laughed and lumbered over, taking Diego in a big embrace before releasing him with a slap on the shoulder that nearly sent Diego toppling over.

"Now get out of here before I decide I want more than a hug." Micky winked, putting his arm around the woman again and walking off as if none of that had happened.

For a long moment Diego stood there, thinking about the significance of the vest and what Lady Woo's actions meant. As far as he could see, there was no way around going to war with her.

# CHAPTER ELEVEN

**Near Trondheim**

The group had finally managed to get the remaining airship working and into the air, and Cammie stood at the prow. She watched the other ship, captained by William, lift and start after them, and soon the two were sailing through the skies toward the north.

Sunlight came in bursts as thick, billowing clouds moved rapidly overhead. The men and women on this ship stared at her, returning to work whenever she caught them. Soon it got old, so she retired to the control room, where the teenage girl, Lillian, stood with the older man.

"Your father?" Cammie asked.

Lillian nodded.

Cammie glanced through the windows at her team of ten, all of them on edge, all of them ready in case there was trouble.

"You know Trondheim well?"

The girl nodded. "Our town is close, but… It's a dangerous place, that whole region. The gods are fierce."

Cammie nodded. "We met some of their wrath on the way over."

JUSTIN SLOAN & MICHAEL ANDERLE

The man frowned, glancing at her and then saying something to his daughter.

"How so?" Lillian finally asked. "Can you explain?"

"Oh, just over the ocean it was crazy. A storm, thunder and lightning, you know? And we lost one of our ships."

Lillian did her best to hide a smile. "No, no, not that kind of gods. The *real* ones."

Cammie frowned, confused.

"Oh, no offense meant." The girl looked horrified. "I mean, if you worship a thunder god, that's not unheard of in these parts. But we're talking about the ones some of the other locals worship, and we've seen them. They're real enough, that's for sure."

"Assuming that's true—that there are gods, real ones—you don't worship them?"

Lillian and her father shared a look of dread, then she shook her head while he cursed in Norwegian and feigned spitting.

"Those gods are, how do you say, *evil*." Lillian glanced at her dad, as if unsure whether to say more. "You're in danger, coming here. It's noble what you're doing, bringing the boy home and all, but you should go."

A land with evil gods? Cammie was already starting to have a good idea of what those gods might be like. She had known enough Weres and vampires in her day to know that some might misuse their powers, and she wouldn't put it past that type to force others to worship them.

What she found hard to understand was how anyone would willingly go along. Well, unless it was a power thing. Perhaps these so-called gods had promised that their most loyal followers could one day become one of them?

That was a scary thought.

"I would like to meet these gods," Cammie told them. "Maybe we could have a bit of a pissing contest, see who wins."

"A...what?"

"Ignore me." Cammie chuckled. "Old habits are hard to break."

A shot rang out, then another, clearly pinging off the airship's hull.

"What the hell was that?" Cammie yelled, already moving for the door as Lillian followed.

The father shouted something and Lillian replied. When she and Cammie were outside, one of their men held a rifle over the side and fired a shot.

"Another ship?" Cammie asked.

One of her sailors, a woman she'd come to know as Trista, had her rifle ready too, but she shook her head. "Just a group on the ground, firing up at us."

"What the hell for?"

"My guess, based on the direction they were heading when we flew past, is that they were going to retrieve their buddies and the airship. And they just figured out that we now have it."

Cammie smiled. "Conserve ammo. They can't touch us as long as we stay high enough that they can't pop our balloon."

Trista smirked, staring at her as if waiting.

"What?"

"Nothing. Just, I'd heard you were notorious for your sexual innuendo jokes, and I figured—"

"That I'd follow up with some sort of 'pop your cherry' joke or something?" Cammie rolled her eyes. "God, a woman has a little fun here and there, and suddenly she's got a reputation."

Trista's eyes went wide. "I didn't mean any offense. I was actually looking forward to it."

"No, you're probably right. I actually should've made a joke there, but the whole Valerie-not-being-back thing is throwing me off." Cammie went to the side of the ship and glanced at the group of shooters below. They were cursing and shouting after them, but had given up trying to take down the airship.

William's ship, with Royland and Kristof on board, was

farther to the east, safely away from the shooters, though she saw a flash of light reflecting from one of the ship's portholes. Then, with a *crack*, one of the men below fell.

These people had been shooting at her ship, so she couldn't blame Royland for taking the shot. It made sense, after all, and those people didn't seem to be on friendly terms with Lillian and her group, who were helping Cammie. So the enemy-of-your-friend rule applied here, but Cammie still felt kind of bad.

Her mind told her heart to shut up and stop whining over it, but the truth was she didn't like the idea of people dying who didn't have to. She was glad to see that no more shots were fired from either group.

"You know them?" she asked, turning back to see Lillian.

She nodded. "Worshipers. Very loyal."

"Well, then, maybe that'll get those gods to show their faces. Get 'em riled up."

"Over the loss of one person?" Lillian shook her head. "They're not likely to care about that, but the fact that foreigners are in their territory is probably reason enough for them to come out and cause some trouble."

"Gods?" Trista asked.

Cammie laughed. "It's a long story. Well, not really. I think there are some Weres nearby proclaiming to be gods."

Lillian's eyes went wide. "How…"

Cammie just smiled. "We've met plenty of their type where we come from, and trust me—they're not gods."

For a long moment Lillian considered her, then pursed her lips in thought. "You aren't here just to return the boy, are you?"

"That would be a long journey just for one lost little boy, wouldn't it?"

"What, then?"

Cammie and Trista shared a hesitant look, but Cammie figured that it could only help to tell this girl as much as she could.

"There was a group of pirates over on the American continent; we had to take them out." Cammie noted that the idea
didn't seem to bother this girl, meaning she was familiar with
the concept of pirates, or whatever that translated to here.
"While one of us was taking down their leaders, she learned
about the groups out this way. And then there was the boy,
telling us that Vikings, or some sort of bandits, whatever, had
taken him from his home and sold him to the pirates in
our area."

"You've come to stop the bandits?" Lillian asked. "I mean, we
don't really call them pirates here, because, like, what year is it?
Vikings and pirates make it feel like we've gone back in time. If
anything, they're a bunch of infantile idiots playing dress-up."

"You *are* familiar with them, then," Cammie said with a wink.
"I couldn't agree more."

"Don't tell Valerie, okay?" Trista added with a chuckle. "I
mean, did you see the way she was dressed?"

Cammie shot her a glare. "Well, she's obviously the exception.
I thought she looked hot as hell in that pirate getup."

Trista nodded, stepping back as if Cammie would strike her.

*Note to self,* Cammie thought. *Don't get too defensive.*

"You have a good shooter on that other ship," Lillian said,
arms crossed, staring out at the other ship. "Hope your friend
doesn't end up using them on us."

"We could've killed all of you within thirty seconds of
meeting you," Cammie assured her. "Trust me, the shooter over
there won't be doing anything rash."

Lillian shrugged. "So you say. We've learned not to trust too
easily."

Soon they were back to simply sailing, the three taking up a
corner of the control room and sharing stories about what it was
like growing up in different parts of the world. Cammie found it
interesting that Lillian had learned to defend herself at such an
early age, but hadn't learned about these gods until they had

come over a few years back. In some ways, she felt, they were very similar.

Trista, however, had been raised by a single dad in the wilderness northwest of Prince Edward Island. She had largely been sheltered, to the extent possible, until the day he didn't come back.

"He...passed away?" Lillian asked.

Trista nodded. "Found his body a couple weeks later as I was tracking a squirrel for food. A bad fall was all it was. He missed one step and my life was turned upside down. For a while I resented him, even more after I'd joined the pirates and learned what my new life would be like. It was the only way I could figure to survive, since he'd never taught me."

Cammie hadn't had anyone to teach her either, though her Were abilities gave her a little help in the survival department.

"Just keep on surviving," she advised. "That's all we can do."

"But it's different now, isn't it?" Trista asked. "I mean, under you and Royland, the island is a different place. A place where we can live without worry, without thinking someone might try to slit our throats in the night, or worse."

"I'd like to think so," Cammie replied, noticing that Lillian's narrowed eyes were slowly losing that look of mistrust.

They went on like this until someone shouted that they had arrived and the captain started working to set the ship down.

Cammie excused herself and went out to get her first glimpse of the city. It was a beauty, and directly on the coast. If this was where Kristof was from, she could see why it would bring back fond memories. Of course, his family being here likely helped in that regard, though that was a concept slightly more foreign to Cammie.

The ship started pulling around and, at first Cammie thought they were turning back. Then she saw that they were simply bringing the airships down outside the city at a spot where there were plenty of surrounding trees, so they wouldn't be out in the open.

"In case there are problems," Lillian noted when she got near Cammie, as if reading her mind. "Thing is, we don't come out this way much, and we never know what we'll find when we do."

Cammie nodded, but her eyes were still glued to the city. As impractical as the thought was, she hoped to catch a glimpse of Valerie walking out to meet them. She hoped her friend had spotted them flying in, or would at least be waiting at some bar in the city with a beer in her hand.

As of yet, however, there was no sign of her.

She went to the other ship to let Kristof know they had arrived, but paused at the sight of Elroy staring up at her with wide, sad eyes.

"What're you doing out here, girl?" she asked, scratching her behind the ears before walking in.

She found Royland and Kristof sitting side by side at the back of the room, staring out one of the portholes.

"And if anyone gives you any crap?" Royland asked.

"Knock him on his ass and warn him to never try it again," the boy replied.

"And if he comes at you again?"

"Get my big buddy the vampire to suck his blood."

"That's right." Royland laughed, gently punching the boy's shoulder. "Just remember everything I taught you, and you'll do fine."

"You sure I can't have one of those sniper rifles?"

"I'm fairly certain that wouldn't go over well. Plus, we only have a limited supply of ammo that works for that type of gun, so…"

Suddenly the boy hugged Royland, who stiffened and glanced at Cammie with a raised eyebrow. She motioned for him to hug back and he did, wrapping his arms around the boy.

"I'm going to miss you," Royland admitted. "Come visit us whenever you want to. You know where we'll be."

Kristof pulled back, smiling but with a tear in his eye. "Singing and dancing on that island?"

Royland nodded. "You bet your ass."

Kristof laughed. "You...you should take the dog. You need her more than I do."

Royland seemed to be seriously considering this offer, but then he took Kristof by the shoulders and said, "I want Elroy at your side at all times. We can't stay, but she can. She's your dog, your friend."

"Oh, thank God!" Kristof laughed. "I regretted the words the second they left my mouth."

"I thought you might," Royland agreed with a fatherly smile. He sighed, then hugged Kristof again and stood. "Take care of Cammie out there, you hear? This is a strange land for her, and you're the big man now."

Kristof rolled his eyes, but nodded.

"Good." Royland hesitated, then added, "I'll miss you."

"I'll miss you, too. Thank you for everything." Kristof turned to Cammie and nodded, and the two of them left.

As they walked past Elroy, she stood and followed them out, her tail wagging the whole way.

"That was kind of you," Cammie told Kristof. "You're going to turn out all right, I can tell."

"Thanks," he replied. "You too."

She laughed and led him the rest of the way up, mentally preparing her own farewell for when the time came.

## CHAPTER TWELVE

**The Badlands**

If there was one thing Diego hated, it was betrayal. Lady Woo had said that if they got El Diablo on their side she would join them. Well, sending people to attack you and make you think it was El Diablo wasn't exactly a sign of good will.

The betrayal hadn't been entirely unexpected, but that didn't make him like it any better. In fact, it irked him even more. At least if it had been unexpected, he could have been mad at himself for not seeing it coming. As it played out, however, he was fully focused on his newfound hatred for this lady and his desire to see her fall.

"You did well," he told Clara and Platea.

Clara scoffed. "I always do," she countered, but then paused, gave him a nod, and added, "Thanks."

"I guess being a pirate comes with a certain amount of knowhow in a fight," Garcia said. "Good thing, too, because it's about to be put to the test."

Wallace let out a deep breath. "Shouldn't we head back to the city and gather more forces for something like this?"

"Not if we want to keep the advantage. Right now they're not sure if their plan worked. They might be sitting there thinking they succeeded, that either we're dead or the people of El Diablo are. If we go back to New York first, they'll have time to check it out before we get back here. Then they'll be ready, and you saw that place. We'll take it, sure, but might lose good soldiers in the process."

"But these two—" he started, pointing at Platea and Clara.

"Stop right there," Platea said, checking her rifle, then holding it close as if he were going to try and take it. "If you're going to say that because we're women you don't see us being part of this, you might just have an ass-kicking headed your way."

Wallace turned to Diego for help, but he just shook his head. "I'm with her on this one, Chief."

"Thank you." Platea glanced at him and smiled. "Nice vest. It suits you."

"He's spoken for," Garcia warned, jealousy clear in his voice.

Platea laughed, moving her foot to touch his. "It's not *that* nice of a vest."

Garcia blushed, and it was Diego's turn to laugh.

"Hey, you two, we're about to go into a fight. No time for that."

"But if we're about to go into a fight and possibly die, maybe—"

"Don't say it!" Clara glared. "Let's just kick some butt and get out of here. When we get back to New York, you can do whatever the hell you want."

Platea smiled and shrugged. "Oh, well. Next time, Sarge."

Diego tried to ignore the googly-eyed look the sergeant was giving her, focusing instead on the quickly approaching base. A flash of light caught his eye from the hill past the base, and then the *crack* of a sniper rifle caught his attention. The bullet pinged off the Pod, reinforcing Diego's belief that Pods were pretty damned badass.

"Get us down, out of sight of those hills," he ordered, but he saw movement as he scanned the area. People were heading down the hill toward the military base. "They must've sent runners as soon as we arrived last time. We have company."

"That can't be right." Garcia scooted up next to him to take a look. "Reinforcements. Damn."

"We're still doing it?" Wallace asked. "It's not too late to back out, you know."

"It's still happening," Diego replied.

They flew the Pod right into the city this time, deciding not to try running in or breaching the gates while getting shot at. He guessed he had been right in assuming they didn't have much in the way of guns, since few shots were fired as they made their descent. Some, but not many.

They exited onto a roof and made their way to the front edge, where Wallace, Platea, and Clara took up defensive positions with rifles while Diego and Garcia headed for the back edge.

Two shots were fired, and a man fell. Diego hadn't even noticed him coming at them, and only now saw the pistol at the man's side.

"Keep it up!" he shouted, then dropped the rest of the way just as more fighters appeared through a doorway. Given the nature of the city they were in a bit of a courtyard, and having the rifles up top was a clear advantage. However, one of the enemy got off a shot that nearly hit its mark. Diego ran forward shouting for them to hold their fire, rolled to an old table that he used for cover, and came up firing. He put two shots into the man's chest.

The only survivors had clubs, so Diego stood, held up a hand to his backup to show he had this, and grabbed his rifle with both hands as they came at him. Parrying one blow with the rifle, he slammed the butt into the man's nose, then used it to uppercut the next man. A final slam into each of their faces with his Were strength put them out of commission.

"None for me, huh?" Garcia asked, catching up as they walked through the door.

"You want some? Diego smiled, gesturing forward. "Take those."

Another group with crowbars, two-by-fours, and knives was moving toward them.

"Just to let you know, we're only here to ask your boss lady what the fuck's wrong with her," Garcia commented. "We do have a slight advantage over you, and don't really want to kill you all."

"Really?" Diego asked. "*I* kind of want to."

"You promised them to me."

Diego laughed. "Well, hurry up, or you're not going to get your chance."

The enemy was almost upon them, so Garcia lifted his rifle and sent a few rounds through the closest ones, then followed Diego's lead by using the rifle itself as a weapon.

Having disposed of this group, they advanced into the main assembly room, pausing briefly at the door as more gunshots rang outside.

"Either my fighters got yours, or vice versa," Lady Woo announced from her dais at the far wall. It had been just an assembly room moments before, but now a partition wall had been moved back to reveal black and white monitors and a small armory—mostly knives and whatnot, but there were a couple of guns.

Her fighters were apparently in the middle of gearing up.

"Let me guess, my men squealed?" she asked, glaring at the closest man as if it were his fault.

"Actually, no," Diego replied. "We figured it out, with the help of my new buddy Micky."

"Those idiots?" Lady Woo waved a hand and her fighters fanned out, forming a half circle around Diego and Garcia to block access to Lady Woo. "They're too gullible, falling for every trick up my sleeve. If you put them in charge of anything, they'll mess it up. That's what inbreeding does, and—"

*BAM! BAM!*

Diego had grown tired of her blathering and opened fire on her guards. Garcia followed his lead, but suddenly more fire sounded from outside, but not just from the direction of the rooftop. It was coming from a distance.

Micky and his team had arrived, or were at least close, and had opened fire on Woo's support in the hills. That was Diego's best guess.

Lady Woo backed up as her team moved in, and bullets started coming back now. Garcia cursed, diving for cover on the other side of the stage, while Diego figured he was done messing around and charged, transforming as he did. Two bullets went right through the spot where he would have been standing in his human form and he pounced, clawing and biting his way through the guards.

A spear—an actual spear—nearly took out his hind legs, but he rolled out of the way and lunged up.

Where was she? He took down another fighter, caught a baseball bat to the side, and transformed back to snatch the bat away and beat the guy with it before realizing Garcia was calling for him.

"Diego! They're being overrun out there!" he was shouting. "We gotta get back to them!"

Diego cursed, grabbing his clothes and running as Garcia provided covering fire.

"Can't you just wear stretchy pants when you think you might have to transform?" Garcia asked as they darted back through the hallway.

"You're just pissed because this isn't working as planned."

"No shit." Garcia turned and fired back the way they'd come. "You get enhanced Were brains too, to figure that out?"

Diego laughed, maintaining his pace as he pulled his clothes back on. They burst back through the front door to see that Wallace and the ladies had moved back toward the Pod and were taking fire. A grenade soared through the air, landed on the edge of the roof, and rolled.

Using all his Were speed, Diego darted forward, leaped to the level of the rooftop, and lobbed it back. It exploded in the air just past the wall.

"Where they hell did they get grenades?" Garcia shouted, already climbing the nearest wall to get back up to the roof. Bullets impacted nearby and he shouted, "I need cover fire!"

Instantly Wallace was there, shooting in the direction the bullets had come from.

"They're proving to be a bit more of a challenge than we had expected," Garcia admitted.

"Then can we get the fuck home for reinforcements?!" Wallace asked. He didn't swear often, and Diego knew he meant business when he did.

He made it onto the roof and returned fire, shooting at a group that had formed behind a hill. Others moved up on the buildings. The shots were coming from both inside the compound and out, and it wasn't looking good.

"We have no choice," Garcia shouted. "Into the Pod!"

Diego cursed, but knew he was right.

The others were in the Pod and he pressed himself against it, firing two more rounds and hitting both his marks. He saw the muzzle flashes of other shots being fired in the hills in the distance.

He jumped in, closed the door, and pointed. "Get us over there, Wallace. That's gotta be Micky."

"And?!"

"And we need to tell them to retreat!"

Wallace glanced back, annoyed, but nodded and took off. They made it there in a matter of minutes, shooting through the open windows at a group trying to take the hill, and slewed past to see Micky and some others holding out at some suburban ruins. The Pod dropped lower and Diego leaned out.

"We need reinforcements!"

Micky pointed down the hill. "They're coming. I wouldn't doubt if more are on the way."

"Can you hole up at El Diablo? Maybe make it to New York?"

Micky cursed, fired two rounds down the hill, and glanced back, thinking about it. "We have too much going on there. We can't leave, not with Pops."

Diego understood. Some health issue, he guessed, that they didn't have time to go into right now.

With a nod, he ordered, "Get back there. We're going for reinforcements, and when I say reinforcements, I mean in a big way. Just...hold out, got it?"

Micky nodded, sounded the retreat, and they were off.

"Pull her around for cover fire," Diego shouted to Wallace. He started to protest, but Diego wasn't hearing it. "JUST DO IT!"

Wallace grumbled again, but turned the Pod down the hill and flew at the attackers. Bullets pinged left and right off the Pod, but stopped once the shots started coming back at them. They rotated twice while firing, hoping to take out enough to provide a good head start for Micky and his crew, then took off for New York.

"It shouldn't have happened like this," Diego mused, staring back at the smoke rising from where the grenade had gone off. It must've lit a fire, he figured. That, or the blaze had been caused by all the other fighting.

"You really expected it to go differently?" Wallace scoffed. "Hate to break it to you guys, but the world we live in doesn't just start suddenly functioning perfectly because we ask it to."

"That's right." Diego pulled himself together, leaning back in his seat. "We're going to have to use a heavy hand."

Garcia nodded. "Force is the only language some of these assholes understand. They want force? They're about to meet a world of pain."

Clara bit her lip. "You guys...you're sure of this? I mean, can't we just walk away?"

"I won't abandon Micky, not after they backed us like that," Garcia argued.

"And I won't abandon America," Diego added.

"With what just happened, they'll talk. A Pod among them, shooting like that? They know we're a real threat, so they'll call the forces of the entire network together, and I imagine most will answer."

Garcia gave Diego a worried look, then nodded. "Tell her what you did back there."

At first he wasn't sure what Garcia meant, but then Diego groaned. "I...might have transformed."

"Well, that does it," Clara sighed, face in her hands. "They'll call on them all, and knowing they're up against Weres, maybe worse if Lady Woo embellishes? Yeah, I'd just say, based on rumors only, of course, we probably won't be the only army with Weres and vampires."

Diego sat up at that. "You're shitting me."

"I wish. Who knows what to believe, but rumor had it there were at least one or two packs in the network, and maybe some of those, what do you call them?"

"Forsaken," Platea chimed in.

"Exactly."

Diego scratched his head, feeling sheepish. This was, at least in part, his fault. He could've handled it differently, but he hadn't. He'd let his temper get the better of him, and now? Now it sounded like they were going to war.

"I can't wait to tell Sandra," he muttered, closing his eyes and just wanting to sink into the seat and never emerge. "Oh God, why am I worried about this when I know she'll kill me first anyway?"

"Because you know she can't," Garcia said. "The baby would be pissed at her if she killed its dad."

"Good point," Diego commented. "Can you maybe stand there and remind her of that when this goes down?"

Garcia laughed and nodded. "Sure, buddy. You can count on me."

The Pod continued its flight over the badlands, leaving the chaos behind for now. Soon, though, all hell was going to break loose.

# CHAPTER THIRTEEN

**Trondheim**

Arriving in Trondheim, Cammie couldn't help but notice that the city seemed to be spooked. Many of the townsfolk were indoors, some glancing at them through shuttered windows as they passed.

It was just her, Lillian and her father, and William, with Kristof and Elroy in the middle in case there was trouble.

"This is your city, yes?" Lillian asked.

Kristof nodded, while Elroy stuck close to him and gave a yip that was almost a bark.

"Just lead us to your house," Cammie told him. Her heart was still breaking over the goodbye between Royland and the boy. It was as if a father had given up his son, and Cammie knew at that moment that something was going to have to change in their lives. Maybe they should get a dog? Maybe, just maybe... She would try to find out if a vampire had any chance of getting a Were pregnant. Even thinking about it made her chest pound. Out of everything she had faced in life, the thought of raising a child was the most terrifying.

If it wasn't possible, though, they would figure something out.

Kristof had gestured that he thought his house was down a side street between two taller houses, but now he paused, clearly lost.

"I've never gone there from this way before," he explained.

"Which way did you go before?" Cammie asked.

Scrunching up his face, he pointed to the water. "We always came and went by boat."

She smiled with relief and motioned for them to all head to the water. She had been starting to worry that they were in the wrong city.

They passed brick houses, some built of wood with chipped paint, and some that were barely houses at all anymore. A couple of very nice-looking ones were visible at the back of the town; Cammie guessed that's where they'd find the town leaders.

Halfway to the water, several men with long jackets and long hair stepped into their path, some with their arms folded, others carrying sticks. One wore a gold bracelet and held a rifle.

"We've got a problem," one in front shared. "See, we don't like strangers in our town, and judging by your exclusive use of the common tongue, we're guessing you aren't from around here."

"You're speaking it too," Cammie argued, eyeing the group to see if she wanted to start trouble. No sign that they were anything other than normal human, at least.

"I speak it when needed." He stared, ice-blue eyes boring into her. "What's your business here?"

"Let them be," another man called from a window.

The blue-eyed man shouted something at him, then pulled a pistol from the back of his pants and aimed it at the man. It had the intended effect; the window emptied immediately.

"Back to what we were saying—"

A brick hit him upside the head, and down he fell. Everyone was looking around to see what had happened when the door of the house where the man had been burst open and he charged forward with two more bricks. The second brick thrown clocked the man with the rifle, hitting him in the neck. He staggered back, holding his throat and cursing, while the other men moved to get the attacker.

Cammie shared a look with Lillian, and saw that her dad had handed her his pistol and held a dagger himself.

Meanwhile, two more men from the town saw what was going on and ran over to help the one who had thrown the bricks, but the thug with the rifle had recovered and was starting to take aim. It had all happened in a blink of the eye, and Cammie knew she needed to stop it.

Instead of waiting for the man to act, she leaped, grabbing the brick, and spun to slam it into the man with the rifle. That was when she caught the whiff… Weres.

Dammit!

Three of the men had already torn off their clothes and transformed into their wolf form, and now the man with the rifle was smiling. He pulled the trigger as she threw the brick, bullet exploding the brick less than a foot from her face.

Two shots took him down, and she turned to see William with his rifle to his shoulder. Lillian was aiming the pistol, but she was shaking and one of the werewolves was going for her.

Elroy was barking like mad and Kristof's voice shook as he told the dog everything would be okay.

Cammie had just started to transform when she thought better of it. They didn't want the other people in his city, the good ones, think that she was one of these so-called gods. *Get in, get Kristof home, and then get back to dealing with the bad guys; that was the goal.*

What would they think of Kristof if he was brought back by a Were?

Instead, she changed only enough to do some damage. She let her claws grow and ran for the wolf that was almost on Lillian, grabbing it by the tail with one hand and yanking to get leverage as she dug her claws deep into its belly, letting its guts spill.

The other wolves turned to her, catching her scent. While half the men had seen that they were in trouble and fled, the other half were engaged in combat with the man from the window and his two helpers.

Lillian finally got a shot off, putting the downed Were out of his misery, and William was trying to get a clean shot without hitting the supposedly good ones.

"Keep Kristof back!" Cammie shouted. Both Lillian and her dad pressed against him, weapons at the ready.

At those words, one of the men from the alley turned and looked at them with wide eyes, only to catch a stick across the face. Cammie had the two Weres to deal with and as William shot one squarely between the eyes, she moved toward the other. A Were got in her way and she took him down, glad to hear the clatter of his stick.

She rolled back, grabbed the stick from the ground, and broke it in two. Just as the wolf reached her, she thrust half of the broken stick through each eye, deep—through bone and into brain—and the wolf fell to the ground, dead.

The man who had been hit in the face was struggling with the guy who had the stick, and there were still two more thugs. When they saw the other Weres down and what they were up against, however, they turned and fled, leaving only the man with the stick.

With a headbutt, the defender broke the other's nose, pulled the stick away, and then whacked the guy in the throat.

"Do we chase them?" Cammie asked.

The man who now had the stick shook his head, looking at the dead Weres in awe. But that wasn't what he cared about, apparently, because a moment later he looked up, searching the defenders, and said, "Kristof? Did someone say—"

"Here," Lillian replied, and cautiously moved aside for them to see the boy.

The reaction was immediate. His stick dropped to the ground

and the man who had thrown the brick ran toward the boy, only to be stopped by Elroy's growling and barking.

"It's okay, I know him!" Kristof told her, kneeling to pet Elroy and hold her back. "It's okay, girl."

"Kristof?" the man said. "Where? How?"

"We...found him," Cammie answered.

"They saved me," Kristof replied. "Then they flew all the way across the ocean to bring me back."

The man shook his head, eyeing Cammie skeptically. "Nobody does that."

She shrugged, feeling sheepish. "Call us old-fashioned, but we cared about a boy being with his family."

"And all this?" He gestured around at the dead. "Not your first time dealing with them, is it?"

She shook her head, not offering anything more than that.

For a moment the man's stare didn't waver, but finally he blinked as if waking from some trance and a smile spread across his face. He turned to one of his buddies and gave him an order, pointing.

As the buddy ran off, the leader said, "Kristof's sister doesn't work very far away, and—"

He didn't even have time to finish the sentence before a young woman came running around the corner, shrieking with joy. She picked up Kristof and spun him around, then put him back down and knelt at his side, hugging him so tightly it looked like she would never let him go. Others were starting to gather as well, looking around to see what the commotion had been.

The man spoke to some of the bystanders, and they quickly started moving the bodies, with Cammie's help. Two more took charge of the one who was still alive, dragging him off to imprison him somewhere, Cammie imagined.

Kristof's sister was speaking with him in Norwegian, but when Cammie passed she looked up at her and put a hand on her arm. "Thank you." She looked at the others, too, lower lip trembling. "From the bottom of our hearts, thank you."

"Yeah, well..."

Cammie was caught off-guard when the sister and Kristof both jumped up and hugged her, then pulled back and let Elroy into their midst, tail wagging. A glance at Lillian showed her trying to hold back tears, and she nodded in approval.

"What'll happen here?" Cammie asked, nodding toward the blood.

Everyone shared nervous glances, but no one spoke.

Finally Lillian cleared her throat. "They were followers of the gods, men sent here to keep the city under control, am I right?"

The man with the stick nodded.

"Then they'll come back with the gods, I imagine. Maybe tonight, maybe in a day, or a week. There will be a reckoning."

"How many of these *gods* are we talking about?" Cammie asked.

The man scrunched his face. "Maybe twenty? Thirty?"

Damn. Without Valerie, Cammie wasn't sure she could handle that many. As her mind raced to find a way to deal with the situation, she agreed to go with the group and get Kristof home.

Soon they had found his house and he was reunited with his whole family. The dining hall was cleared out at the local church so that the whole city could celebrate Kristof's return.

"You must stay for the feast tonight," Kristof's father told them. "Get everyone else from the ships—Lillian told me there were more—and bring them. It'll be glorious!"

Cammie was about to refuse, but then she remembered it actually made sense to stay. If the gods sent just a few Weres, she and her sailors could help defend the city. That, and it was the one place they were expected to be, and Valerie knew that.

*She would have to come through here, right?*

"Deal," Cammie agreed, smiling.

When the man had left to see to his son again, William asked what she was thinking.

"The plan is to wait for Valerie," Cammie replied, then turned to Lillian. "Where are these gods, in relation to here?"

"Not far to the east," Lillian answered.

"And the closest town of theirs? I mean, with the largest number of their followers?"

"West, actually."

"See?" Cammie gloated, looking at William. "We're right in the center. She'll go for one of those two. We wait the night and help defend if necessary. She'll be here."

"Unless she's totally lost," he argued. "I mean, with all this nature around us, the idea isn't completely improbable."

"You clearly haven't known Val as long as I have." She started walking back to the ship. "Come on, let's tell the others that they're invited to a celebration. I, for one, am looking forward to it."

And she really was. They had accomplished the half of the mission she cared most about, and was certain Valerie would find them by the night's end.

During the feast Cammie constantly found her eyes wandering to the door of the great hall, hoping for any sign of Val, but she couldn't deny the fun of the evening.

The feast and celebration were out of this world. Everything was different here, from the way they made lemon-baked cod, sprinkled with paprika, to their buried salmon, which confused Cammie but was to die for. As the first couple of courses came to an end, a husky man brought out an instrument they called a fiddle. It produced music that was very different from the banjo back on the island, but the excitement and dancing had a very familiar feel.

*A home away from home*, she thought. If there was a place she could live away from America, she could certainly see this being it.

After nightfall, Royland and a few of the others from the ship came, though they had promised the ones left on watch that they would switch out at some point to give them a chance to celebrate.

"This is them," Kristof said, stepping up next to them with a tall, warrior-looking man at his side. His stark-blonde hair was slicked back, and he sported a red beard and a smile that made you feel at ease.

"My little brother's saviors," the man exclaimed, clapping Royland on the shoulder and then taking Cammie's hand and shaking it vigorously. "The name's Christian, by the way."

"Brother?" Royland asked, looking Kristof's way.

"Technically, no," Kristof said.

Christian laughed. "But in my heart, he'll always be my little brother. When we thought we'd lost him, I went after the men who took him...and got this instead."

He pulled up the leg of his pants to reveal a wooden leg.

Kristof looked shocked at first, but then smiled. "It does make him look more exciting though, doesn't it?"

Cammie laughed. "It certainly does."

"Where are the men who did this to you?" Royland was far from laughing. He was glaring at the wooden leg.

Christian let the pant leg fall back down and considered the vampire. "What, you are going to deliver Kristof to us and then rid our little corner of the world of evil too?"

Royland slowly nodded. "Yes, I hope we can do exactly that."

For a long couple of beats, Christian stared, lips pursed. Then he lifted his drink. "Well, cheers to that!" Chucking his cup to the side, he smiled widely. "Just don't get yourself killed out there."

"They can handle themselves, Brother," Kristof said, serious as hell.

"Can they? Against the supposed gods?" Christian assessed Royland and Cammie again, then nodded. "Hell, I don't know your secrets and don't need to, but I have to warn you that this isn't just some local group of thugs. These guys... It's like the devil himself possessed their leader, and each of his followers is a demon with the strength of ten men."

Royland nodded. "Which way?"

Christian nodded to one of the large windows to their right. "East, slightly northeast. You'll find the gods out there...or they'll find you."

With a glance at Cammie to see if she objected, the vampire said, "We'll do what we can, if our friend hasn't already. But for now, I see a pretty woman over there who can't seem to keep her eyes off you."

"Her?" Christian nodded. "You could consider this our honeymoon, though I hope to do better soon. Just married."

Kristof hit him. "You didn't tell me!"

"You only just returned," Christian countered in his own defense. "Come, let us celebrate. Talk of gods and death can be put off until afterward."

They returned to the merriment, and Cammie couldn't help but have an amazing time. It was helped by the fact that Royland was practically beaming. He had thought his farewell with Kristof on the ship would be the last time he saw the boy, but here they were, having the time of their lives. She was pretty sure that if it were possible, returning in the future wouldn't just be a possibility but a necessity.

It was a night Cammie wished would have never ended, in part because she was so sure Valerie would arrive. When that didn't happen, she was left very confused.

As she finally drifted off to sleep in that great hall, she told herself there was still hope. They would be up with the sunset, and would set off immediately to find her.

CHAPTER FOURTEEN

**Meldal**

Valerie's journey to Meldal lasted two hours, though most of that was due to the mountainous terrain. She had no problem moving fast, but had to watch her footing to avoid falling.

Soon she found herself jogging past green fields that were squared off in what had once been farmland. The city looked normal, although it didn't have much water around aside from a river due to its higher elevation. A gray church steeple rose above the other buildings, and she found herself enjoying the architecture of the old buildings.

She walked right into town, not waiting to see if the people would address her or attack when they saw her. She knew it had been their ships she had downed the night before, their people she had killed. They would be weakened, confused.

So when she saw a man pushing a wheelbarrow of beets and potatoes down the street, she simply smiled and kept walking. He stared at her in shock, then quickly ran into a nearby building.

Her hope was that he would alert the others, because she really didn't want to drag this out any longer than necessary. A sign caught her attention and she paused, staring at it. The wooden carving of a wolf hung above the door, its eyes painted red. Now that she had noticed it, the signs were everywhere. More wolves, some painted on canvas near a bakery, in a very rustic style.

Many buildings had laundry drying from lines tied between them, sheets flapping in the wind, and she wondered if the overall darkness in the city was natural or an effect of the overcast sky.

"Something you like there?" a woman asked, and Valerie turned to see a woman in her mid-thirties, wearing a thick fur coat. She was covered in tattoos, but they were not random designs. Hers were intricately patterned such as one would expect to see in old Norse paintings, only each had the common theme of a wolf.

Valerie nodded. "Very much so."

"Are you...familiar with our ways? You don't sound local."

"Some of my best friends are wolves, as a matter of fact. But no, I hear you have a different approach than I do."

"Approach? We simply recognize power where power resides, and respect it. If gods have been born among us, we raise them to the position of authority they deserve."

"Ah, then I'm in the right place. If you all appreciate power, well...seeing as you already know about the supposed Unknown-World, here's what I'd like to do." She let her eyes turn red, then smiled as her fangs grew long. "Tell me where I might find these so-called gods of yours, then stop worshiping them and never attack innocents or partake in piracy or banditry again."

The lady blinked, caught totally off-guard, and took a step back. "What are you?"

"The Enforcer of Justice. I've sailed across the ocean to ensure innocents are safe and reclaim honor for my kind, but I've heard tales of wrongdoing by your people. Have I been misinformed?"

She took another step back, eyes darting to the doorways of

the nearby buildings from which other men and women were emerging. Valerie sensed their fear and hostility, and she could smell their steel. They were coming to fight.

"You sent out fighters yesterday." Valerie spoke loudly enough for those nearby to hear. "They won't be returning."

"And why is that?" This time it was a man who asked. He had tattoos much like the woman's, but the designs covered his face as well. He even had red wolf eyes tattooed above his eyebrows.

"They attacked. They were killed."

"By you?"

"By me." Valerie turned, letting them all see what she was. "Tell your gods I'm here and I'm waiting. It's either that or I send them a message myself, though I have to warn you that mine will be written in blood."

"The gods grant us their powers," the man snarled, quickly popping something into his mouth.

Valerie was pretty sure that it was the drugs she had already experienced. It started to click now—they worshiped the Weres because they wanted to *be* them. Maybe they could earn their place, prove themselves. The Weres had promised that they would convert them, give them their powers. In the meantime, these people were granted extra strength by their gods, strength that came from this drug.

"If you're going to come at me now, I have to warn you—your friends took the drug too. It didn't help them."

"I don't believe you." The man scoffed. "When they return, we'll roast your corpse for dinner and see if you taste half as bad as the shit coming out of your mouth."

"Hmm." Valerie smiled. "I think you'll serve as a perfect example for the rest here."

The man sneered, then pulled a battleax from the doorway behind him and charged.

She waited until the last minute, then moved aside. The

battleax sliced past her and split a support beam on the nearby store in half. With her claws, she tore large gashes in his cheek.

"Just a test, because I'd love to know. You didn't feel that?"

The man turned with a roar and came at her again.

"I'll take that as a no," she declared, again moving out of the way of his attack. This time she kicked out his knee. "I don't have to kill you. Ask my friends. They'll vouch for my generous nature."

She kicked him down and he pushed himself up again, trying to stand but flopping backward.

"Just tell me you give up, and introduce me to your gods." Valerie took a step back, shaking her head with pity as the man lunged and fell again. "It's as simple as that."

A grunt sounded behind her and she smelled the thick odor of grilled meat and flowers—an odd combination—before the tattooed woman from before charged, thrusting with a short but wide blade.

Valerie sidestepped, then kicked out with her foot and sent the woman plunging right into the downed man, her sword piercing his good leg.

"Ouch! Good thing you can't feel that." Valerie saw others moving in, weapons at the ready. "I didn't come here for violence, necessarily. You all would probably throw rocks at a dragon and be surprised when it breathed its fire upon you. Well, my flames are getting real fucking hot, so back the hell up."

Two men shouted at her in Norwegian, another in a language that sounded different but which she could tell was related. The man at her feet tried to lunge despite that fact that neither of his legs worked, and she took another step back, glancing over to see that the woman had backed away, less certain now.

"I'm going to assume you understand me." Valerie addressed the two men who had yelled. "And I'm going to hope that you want to live to see tomorrow, so I'll tell you one more time. Inform the gods that I'm here. Change your ways."

The man on the ground threw his battleax at her, but she moved her head and it clattered on the cobblestones behind her.

"This one has answered for you all," she stated, then stepped up and kicked him across the face so hard that his head snapped. He fell back to the ground, limp. "Will the rest of you give the same response?"

Several hesitated, and the tattooed woman just put her hand to her mouth and took another step back. After a moment, she turned and ran.

"Coward!" one of the men shouted after her, while several others put the drugs into their mouths.

"I get it. You'd would rather die than face the changing ways of this world," Valerie proclaimed with a sigh. "I just wish it didn't have to be at my hand so often. But if it must be so..."

She drew her sword. "Let's get on with it, shall we?"

The men charged. In their furs and with their tattoos, they almost looked like a pack of wild animals closing on their prey. Of course, in this case it was more like a bunch of stupid lemmings running into the mouth of their predator.

Valerie wasn't going to waste any time. She darted through her attackers, sword a blur of steel, blood flowing in artistic sprays that dappled the ground in patterns that, Valerie thought, worked quite well with all the wolf symbols and patterns around the town.

Soon there was a pile of bodies behind her, forming a semi-circle as if to enclose her own mini-arena.

It wasn't pleasant to have been the creator of this work of art, but she recognized its intimidation factor. She turned, sword at rest, and held out a hand, palm up.

"Was this how you wanted your day to go?" She shook her head in dismay. "I sure as hell didn't."

"You attacked us!" a young man in a thick bearskin coat shouted.

"WRONG!" She pointed, finger shaking with fury at that

comment. "You people in your airships came after me and mine. *I* came here to discuss how we could live in peace, how the world could move forward without bloodshed, without people getting hurt." She gestured to the dead. "This was your answer."

The man glared, chest heaving, and then he dropped his ax. For a moment the others looked at him in confusion, but then their weapons clattered to the ground as well. As one, they knelt and bowed their heads.

"Forgive us," the man implored. "We didn't realize you were one of them."

"One of... Oh, no."

"Yes." The man bowed even lower. "We know better than to attack the gods, but we failed today. We failed to recognize you in this form. In the form of...a woman."

She rolled her eyes. "For fuck's sake, I'm not a god or a goddess, and neither are the Weres you worship."

He looked up at her, brow creased in confusion. "How...how can you say that? We've seen what you can do. There's no denying your divine power."

She scrunched her nose at that, then shook her head. "Stand! All of you, just fucking *stand*."

They did so in one quick motion, as if obeying a god rather than simply following her advice. Dammit.

"Listen closely, because I don't often tell people this." She put away her sword and wiped the blood from her hands on the back of her pants. "I am a vampire. What you worship, those Weres? They are simply humans. But we are what we are not because demons or gods changed us, and certainly not because we *are* gods. We are nothing more than modified humans. We have something in our blood that you do not, something that came, believe it or not, from up there." She pointed to the sky, then shook her head, realizing that could mean the heavens. "Not up there as in gods or God, but as in space. Other beings reside up there, among the stars. I know this is a lot to swallow and you have no real reason to believe me, but that's the truth."

The man stared at her and the others fidgeted, casting cautious glances at each other.

Finally he relaxed and cocked his head, analyzing her. "A vampire?"

She nodded.

"And we shouldn't be afraid of you because?"

"Because vampires and Weres are nothing like the legends of old say they are. As I explained, we are nothing more than genetically modified humans. More than that, I have been given a mission to bring justice to our world. Well, specifically what was called North America long ago, and will be again, but it's flexible. We're restoring this world as best we can. I'd like you all to be a help in that mission, rather than a hindrance."

The man glanced at the remaining townsfolk and warriors, then nodded.

"I'm with you. The others can choose for themselves, but I'll be honest... I've always had my doubts." He fidgeted now, eyes nervous. "But the thing is, they'll come. The fact remains that they call themselves gods and will destroy anyone who says otherwise. If we stand with you, can you protect us?"

"You bet your ass I can."

He blinked, confused by that turn of phrase.

With a laugh, she clarified, "That means 'yes.' How many of them are there?"

"A few dozen, at least," he said.

"Hans," one of the men said, addressing him and then speaking in Norwegian. Hans replied in kind, then turned back to Valerie.

"The others are concerned you'll get us all killed. They've seen your power, but don't believe that means you'll stand up against the gods, er, Weres, for them."

Valerie considered this, looking around at the scared faces.

"Allow me, if you will, to shed some light on my powers and why you have no reason to be afraid." She smiled at the excitement of this moment, having never really put on a display of her powers. Part of her said to stop showing off, to just shut up and go kill the Weres, but she also knew the show would help these people. It would reassure the ones who wanted to follow her and put the necessary fright into the hearts of those who still considered her their enemy.

With a deep breath, she *pushed* just enough fear to cause them to clench their butt cheeks to avoid shitting themselves, then drew her sword and moved as she rarely did when not worried for the life of someone close to her. She was likely a blur in their eyes, a blur of moves, but she paused here and there, sword extended in various positions she had learned during her training in France.

Each time she let them see her she received another gasp from the crowd, finishing in a flurry of moves just slow enough for them to follow, eyes flaring red and teeth fully extended.

"Those Weres are so fucked," the man exclaimed, a smile taking over his face.

Others stared with jaws hanging open, while a few started to cheer and applaud.

She felt like such a turd at that moment. She was the world's biggest showoff. However, her actions seemed to have had their intended effect, so she just nodded, put her sword back in its sheath, and curtsied to them in a fun way that she hoped would show them she wasn't all about swords and death.

A woman disappeared and returned with a fine fur coat a moment later. "For you." She presented it across her arms.

"No, I couldn't." Valerie tried to refuse, but when the woman held it out, she couldn't help run her hand across the smooth fur. *Damn*, she wanted that coat.

"We insist." The man stepped up next to her. He shouted something over his shoulder, and another person ran into the building opposite, returning moments later with a fine belt with a hook for her sword. "Yours looks slightly worn."

She glanced down, noticing for the first time how ragged her belt was.

"Please, it would be an honor to us," the man stated, lowering his voice. "To accept means you are one of us, in a sense. Our protector."

That hadn't been her intention at all when she had set out for this town, but she had learned a long time ago that sometimes it made sense to just roll with it. She nodded and accepted the coat, then dropped her old belt and put on the new one. The sword hung perfectly, and she had to admit that it didn't pull on her hips as it had with the old belt.

"You're too kind." Spinning, she almost giggled. "How do I look?"

"Like a hero straight out of the old books, here to defend us against the evils of the world." The man was likely joking, but something he had said got her attention. "Old books?"

"We have a whole library full of them," he confirmed. "Come, I'll show you."

Before he turned to lead the way, he gestured to the bodies and shouted something in Norwegian. Several men and women nodded and moved toward the corpses.

"They'll...take care of the mess."

She pursed her lips and shook her head. "I wish it hadn't come to that."

"We all feel the same, I'm sure, but sometimes a garden needs to be weeded."

"One day we won't have so many weeds on this earth. One day."

He gave her a wistful smile and motioned for her to follow. They went toward the back of town, past the church she had seen on the way in, to a large building behind it. When they entered she was hit by an old, musty smell, but it was beautiful. More books than she had ever seen in her whole life lined the walls. She felt like jumping onto the wheeled ladder and riding past them while dragging her fingertips across their bindings, but instead she just smiled and breathed it in.

"It's wonderful," she said.

The man nodded. "My collection, you could say. Not all of us are cultureless cave men."

"I'm glad," she admitted. "And pretty damn happy I didn't have to kill you."

"Me too!" he agreed with a hearty laugh. "Some of those men you killed were like family—the kind you hate, if you know what I mean. It's not like everyone would accept you right away, but I imagine you won't be staying long anyway."

"Correct. I plan on dealing with your little werewolf infestation and leaving. I have to find my friends, but if I hear you have gone back to your old ways, I might have to return."

He shook his head. "No, taking care of the Weres should deal with that tendency. There are other communities like ours, but the majority of us were operating out of fright or greed more than true worship. The ones who continue to fight will be dealt with, I imagine. I know I plan on doing my part."

She ran her hands through the fur of her new coat again, glancing around at the books.

"There might just be hope for us all. If we can separate the rotten apples from the barrel, that is."

With that, she pulled off the coat and draped it over her arm.

"What're you doing?" he asked.

"Preparing. I'd hate to get Were blood on the fur."

He laughed, and with that she walked back outside, lodged an ax into a wooden post, and hung her coat on it. Next she sat down cross-legged in the main street and waited for the Weres. She needed to replenish her energy a bit after that display she had put on, so she closed her eyes and waited.

A cool breeze tossed her hair and she felt the sun break through the clouds, if only for a moment.

She focused her breathing, clearing her mind of all negativity. Too much killing. Too many dickheads in this world.

But she had hope. She had faith.

And she had her badass sword to help change it all.

# CHAPTER FIFTEEN

**Meldal**

It came as no surprise that the Weres didn't arrive until well into the night. As far as Valerie knew, they had never dealt with vampires and didn't know that many *preferred* the night. They probably also knew that she had attacked during the day, which by most definitions would mean that she couldn't be a vampire.

Day-walking vampires were rare in every corner of the world. Either way, they were ill-prepared.

She hadn't moved from her spot in the center of town, so when they strolled in wearing their trench coats and fur caps, acting every bit the gods they thought they were, that was where they found her.

It was hard not to laugh at the one who approached her first, with his long gold necklaces and bracelets, leather coat, and thick eyebrows. He must've thought himself some sort of gangster before they had decided he was a god and adorned him with so much jewelry. Now he looked every bit the part of a straight-up douchebag.

Valerie held back her laugh and calmly stood instead, waiting for him to speak.

To his credit, he didn't bother. He simply swung a knife at her.

She preferred directness.

Instead of having to beat him with words, she maneuvered out of the way, grabbed his wrist, and bent it back far enough to make him roll with it. When he was on his back, she stepped forward and snapped the wrist.

He let out a long howl of pain and the others moved forward, brandishing knives.

"Please, join your friend here," she invited them. "I would love nothing more."

"Who the hell do you think you are?" the Were on the ground growled.

"I'm the one who's going to prove to everyone watching that you're no god, simply a man who bleeds and dies like the rest of us. But first I'd like to give you a chance to live. Bring me to your den, introduce me to the head Were, and I'll decide your fate then, along with that of the rest of the Weres here."

"I have a counterproposal," he spat. "I take a chunk out of that pretty face of yours and maybe you die, or maybe I keep you around for breakfast tomorrow."

He twisted and transformed to a wolf, for which she was glad. For some reason it was much easier on her to kill when her opponent looked less human.

Before he had a chance to attack she was on him, one hand on his upper jaw and one on the lower.

"Weres aren't invincible," she informed the crowd watching from their windows and doorways, cautious about getting too close yet wanting to see her fight. "Observe."

She pulled the jaws apart and they snapped, then flesh tore and blood flew as the Were fell, dead. She had ripped his head in two.

A Were cursed in Norwegian and ran forward, and two more joined the charge. More behind them took the drug, then they ran forward too. The approaching Weres tore off their coats and other garments and transformed halfway to her.

The first to reach her got a nice surprise as she took a defensive stance with her claws out, teeth bared, and eyes glowing fiercely. *Pushing* fear, she hissed and moved in for the attack.

The poor Were whimpered like a pup, and by the time she had drawn her sword and cleaved his head in two, the others were reacting as well.

Those in wolf form arranged themselves in a semicircle around her, pausing in their assault while the ones in the back ran for cover. Others still in human form pulled out rifles and pistols, along with one crossbow.

Shots rang out, but Valerie was too fast to be hit—she used the noise as a distraction to dart to her right and flank the first shooter. Her sword sank into his shoulder and she caught the gun as he dropped it.

With a backward thrust to finish him, she lifted the pistol and put two bullets into the head of the next one, then shot a third that was leaping for her. She amped into vampire speed again, cutting down two more and shooting another three before emptying the first gun.

There were two more guns at her feet, but she really preferred her sword.

A werewolf was at her side, about to leap, when she lifted the sword and brought it straight down into his head, pinning it to the ground.

She pulled the sword out as one of them shouted, "Retreat!"

Another argued, but she cut him through and the rest fled.

"I don't think so," Valerie hissed, and then ran down the closest one, grabbing him by the tail and unexpectedly pulling it right off with her strength. She finished him off when he spun on her, but it was more of a mercy kill at that point.

"What the fuck *is* she?" one of them shouted to the apparent leader, but she didn't give him time to answer.

She was at the leader's side in a split-second, smiling to show her teeth, and replied for him. "Vampire, Justice Enforcer, and all around nice gal." She sliced into the leader, cutting him in half before tearing off his head. "I like long walks by the water and nice strolls with my victims before I sink my blade into their faces. What are you?"

"Fucking terrified," he said, and she believed him.

The others stopped running, though they were staring at her in horror as they continued slowly backing away.

"Where's your den?" she asked. "I want to speak with the head god. The God? Whatever you call him."

"You tell her, I'll kill you myself," one of the others said, so she causally threw her sword to lodge in the guy's skull. His eyes moved up to process it, and he fell back with a thud.

She glanced at the others, some lifting their rifles again, others preparing to attack.

"If you think I'm vulnerable because I'm unarmed, you're stupider than you look."

"Say we aren't gods," the Were in front of her said. "Say we take you to our den. What's to stop you from killing all of us right then and there? Wouldn't the smart move be to just let you kill us now and get it over with, if you're as powerful as you claim to be?"

She thought about it, then nodded. "Yes, but then I'd make you hurt more. And here's a secret... I might let you—and only you—live if you turn against the rest of these bunny-munchers and help me."

A moment's hesitation went through his eyes while the others laughed. Their laughter turned into a nervous chuckle, then shouting as the Were she was talking to turned on the one next to him, transforming and biting through the man's jugular.

"This's going to be fun," Valerie shouted, then gave a warcry and turned to take down the ones closest to hurting her newest buddy.

Would she have to watch her back, considering how fast he had turned on his friends? Of course. But her goal right now was to keep one of the so-called gods alive long enough to take her to the den, so she could deal with the grand master of Weres in this area. The Alpha. She didn't give a damn about making long-term friendships.

She had just taken down two and reclaimed her sword when a crossbow bolt hit one of the others. A glance to see where it had come from revealed more townsfolk approaching, weapons in hand. Having seen how easily their supposed gods fell, they were rallying in force.

That made her day.

"Good of you to join," she shouted to Hans, and he saluted her before taking cover around the corner of a house and aiming at another Were.

She didn't leave much work for them, but let them get in enough shots to feel like they'd contributed. Then she finished the others off, all except her new pal.

He had a bolt through his arm and a bullet in his stomach, but those wounds would heal easily enough. Ignoring his yelp as she pulled the bolt free, she motioned for him to lead the way.

"Your coat!" Hans shouted after Val.

"Hold on one second," she told the Were, and jogged back for her coat. When she turned to follow him, he was running for it. She just laughed, expressed her appreciation to the town, and slipped the coat on as she ran after him.

For a while, she let him think he was actually getting away.

When he glanced back for the fourth time with eyes full of terror, she decided it wasn't fun anymore.

"Boo!" she shouted, leaping forward and landing next to him.

The surprise in his eyes was priceless, but then he fell sideways, rolling down a small incline and hitting his head on the tree. "*Fuck!*"

"Watch your mouth. There's a lady present."

He rubbed his head, glaring up at her. "You've got some issues, I'm guessing."

"How so?"

"I mean you're crazy."

"Probably." She jumped down next to him and offered him a hand. "Kept you alive, and that was pretty wacky of me. I talk too much during fights, I've been told. Maybe that's crazy."

"What's crazy is you wanting to take on Barskall."

"Barskall?" she asked, gesturing for him to keep walking beside her.

"Jon Barskall, actually, but he makes us call him General Barskall. Comes from the Barskall family in Iceland, along with many of us. We figured we could set up this little cult thing with the locals. Kinda brilliant."

She glared at him.

"Oh, I mean…not brilliant at all. Horrible, really."

"I'm guessing he has something to do with this power drug everyone's on?"

The Were nodded. "Something his family has been growing for the black market in Iceland. Part of why his father rose to power, if you ask me."

She nodded, catching on. "So, some new power rises, putting this drug on the market, and the brilliant son figures he'll go off and use his Were powers for an extra bit of evil in some other country, is that it?"

"Sounds about right."

"Am I going to have to worry about his family? I mean, with this trans-Atlantic piracy and whatnot?"

"Not that I'd think. They stick to their own, which was one reason the General wanted to spread his wings." The Were considered her, then turned back to watch his step. "Seems you have your hands damned full if you're going to take care of all the problems in the world."

"I'm not the only one out there doing this," she told him,

though she had to admit to herself that what he had said struck a chord. The thought had been at the back of her mind lately, though she hadn't wanted to acknowledge it. Was going from problem to problem the best way to make the world a better place?

Hell, eventually the problems would just pop back up where she had already solved them, and she'd find herself in an endless loop. But certain problems were big enough to worry about, and a den of Weres that proclaimed themselves gods certainly fit the bill.

"Name's Berg, by the way," the Were said.

"What?"

"Just, you haven't asked, so figured I'd tell you. Way I see it, you haven't asked because maybe you'll find it easier to kill me if you don't think of me as a person. So now you have to, right? Think of me as a person, that is."

Valerie scoffed. "Let me put it like this, Berg. I imagine there are quite a lot of things you've done in the not-so-distant past that you regret, or maybe you don't, but others would frown on them, am I right?"

The nervous look in his eyes said it all.

"Exactly." She had to pause to leap a few rocks, while he climbed behind. When he had caught up, she continued, "Now, given everything you've done and the way you yourself have probably said you aren't exactly human—you know, with all this god talk—well, why should a name mean anything to me?"

He gulped and gave a half-hearted chuckle as if he hoped she were joking, and then his face went pale.

"Roger that. But assuming I help you here and don't stab you in the back, forgetting for the moment that you're super-fast and strong and I probably couldn't even if I wanted to, what then? Do you let me live?"

She smiled. "We'll have to wait and see. But know this—I'm not the type to kill just because."

He nodded. "Glad to hear it. Not totally at ease, but I'll take what I can get."

They continued to climb the hill, maneuvering around rocks and between trees, and Berg told her all about the situation so far. He downplayed his role in the whole gods business, of course, but he knew enough of the details for her to guess he had been a lot more involved than he was saying. She would have to watch him, regardless of how much faster and stronger she was. For hours they traveled, soon able to see the water to their left along with a city Valerie thought was likely the one her friends would have gone to.

*Just a little bit longer,* she thought, *then I will get back to them.* They walked for at least another hour, though. It was well into the night when he finally stopped.

"That's us," he finally said, pointing out what looked like an old military base. "The Den of the Gods. Home, sweet home."

"You're kidding?" She wasn't sure what she had been expecting. A hideout carved into the side of a hill like a wolf's den or something? This was almost like a little town, but with metal gates and buildings that all matched. Nothing godlike about it.

"We found the old armory and a few of the guns still worked, so we figured, might as well take that as a sign," Berg offered. "Plus, the General likes the familiar."

"That's good, because me and him are about to get real familiar." She thought about it for a moment, then shook her head. "No, that doesn't sound right. How about this one? I hope he's familiar with a good ass-kicking, because he's about to receive one."

She looked at Berg, who actually smiled. "Hey, I'm just glad I finally found your weakness. On-the-fly witticisms."

"Fuck you. Is that witty enough for you?"

"Honestly, no, but I don't want you to kill me, so…yes."

She laughed. "Seriously, go shoot yourself in the face."

He frowned.

"Okay, not seriously." Valerie motioned to the base. "You can save that for after we take the base."

"We?"

"Yes, clown. You don't think you came all this way just to keep me company, did you?" Noting the fear in his eyes, she added, "You just point me in the right direction. I'll block the bullets and whatnot, keep you alive. You'll go from company-keeper to tour guide."

"Fuck my life."

"Let's hope that doesn't happen." The two of them knelt as he drew a map of the base in the dirt so they could discuss attack plans. Who knew? If all went well, maybe she would keep this guy around.

CHAPTER SIXTEEN

**Den of the Gods**

In the end, Berg and Valerie decided on a slightly different approach than they had originally intended. While she still liked the idea of sneaking in and going all assassin on their asses, there was something to be said for grandiose entrances and simply confronting your problems head on.

Besides, she had done the sneaking-around thing before. Here, she thought she should play to the Weres' fancy.

They wanted to be gods?

Well, she would give them the goddess of all goddesses. It was time to present them with a taste of their own medicine.

"Are you sure about this?" Berg asked as they made their descent to the military compound looming before them. Soon the guards would notice, and there'd be no going back.

She nodded confidently. "If you get into trouble, make your way back to Meldal. I'll try to meet up with you there. If it doesn't work out...sorry."

"Sorry?" He scoffed, then looked to see if she was joking. "I hope you can do a lot better than 'sorry.'"

"Me too." She offered him a reassuring smile, but he didn't seem to be buying it.

With a group of delusional bullies like this, the only tactic she had ever found to work was intimidation. It was that or slaughter every last one of them, but she preferred to have faith that not all of them were completely evil.

He took a deep breath, eyed her warily, and prepared himself mentally. When he finally focused his eyes on the gates ahead, he had a different look to him: stronger, a man you didn't want to mess with.

"The Goddess is here!" Berg shouted from in front of her, leading the way to the gates. "Move aside! The Goddess has arrived!"

It was hard enough not to laugh at him, but seeing the confusion in the eyes of the gate guards was just too much. The corner of her mouth turned up in a way she had to imagine gave her the look of a crazy person. Well, if a goddess *were* coming through like this, perhaps she would have a hint of a smile? *Why not?* she thought, and rolled with it.

She walked tall, fur coat trailing behind her like a cape in the heavy wind. Berg had adorned her with some of his jewelry. With her glowing red eyes and the slight fear she was *pushing* at them, she couldn't imagine that they had ever seen anyone more godlike in their lives.

"I am the Goddess of Justice, here to claim my due," she shouted in a stern voice. It took everything in her not to burst into laughter, and while this was a serious matter, she figured there wasn't a lot of point to life if you couldn't enjoy it. "Bring your master to me, that he may bend his knee and pay me what is rightfully mine."

"What the fuck is this, Berg?" one of the guards asked, and before the other guard understood what was happening, Valerie had leaped forward and kicked out both guards' knees from behind so that they knelt to her. Aside from the beating their knees had taken they were relatively unharmed, and tossed their rifles aside.

"Was that so difficult?" she asked with a wink.

The guards looked at each other, then stood and ran away from the compound.

"You've got a hell of a way of making an entrance," Berg remarked, nodding to show he was impressed.

"We aren't done yet."

Berg sighed, opened the gate, and led her into the compound while continuing to announce her coming.

"The Goddess of Justice! Welcome your Goddess, and bow before her!"

Two wide doors opened in a building to their left, from which half-a-dozen Weres exited. They looked like thugs ready to close a shop, but at least half of them appeared to be as confused as they were angry.

"The circus in town?" a Were at the front of the group asked. He was a small man, short, and covered in so much hair it was probably the hairiest a man could be before transforming into a wolf. "I'd know, and I wasn't told of any circus."

A couple of the others laughed, and he turned on them. "I get to laugh at my jokes, not you."

When he faced Valerie again, she had taken two quick steps to close the gap between them. "Bow."

"I'm a god, bitch. I don't—"

She picked him up and threw him against the building so hard he slammed into its side with an *ooomph* and collapsed to the ground.

"Next," she said, turning to the other five.

"I'd do as she says," Berg advised, but the front two drew batons on her.

Big mistake.

She grabbed their weapons in an instant, beating them mercilessly with the rods. When they'd had enough and tried to crawl away, she turned to see the other three bowing.

"Huh, it actually works." She tossed the batons aside. "Good. Follow me if you want to live."

As Berg once again led the way, she heard mumbling in Norwegian behind her, but a quick glance from her red eyes shut them up.

She could guess what they were saying—let the main one, this General Barskall, deal with her. She looked forward to it.

Berg led her into an old warehouse filled with training dummies, obstacle courses, and more. Weres trained on various courses and weapons. Some, she saw, were even using real knives as they sparred.

At his announcement they turned to stare, totally flabbergasted by what they were seeing, which was her, with her new retinue. She kept thinking they would attack at any moment, but no one did. Glancing around at their faces, she could almost imagine herself in a place just like this back in France under the Duke.

Back with Donovan and the others.

With Sandra at her side.

Her smile faltered just as Berg reached the far side of the warehouse and led her out into a grand courtyard. This place couldn't have been here in the days before the collapse. It was obviously a worship hall or storage place for the offerings and stolen goods they had collected over the years. Tall statues of gold, wooden carvings of wolves, and piles of what could only be described as treasure filled the space.

They might not call themselves pirates like the corny sons of bitches back home, but for all intents and purposes, they were.

At the opposite side was an old general's house. All of the Weres had followed them out of the warehouse and were staring up at the balcony of this house.

Berg glanced back at her nervously, but she nodded for him to go on. "The Goddess of Justice demands you submit to her, bend your knee, and..." He looked back again, really not wanting to say this last part. She gave him a nod, so he shouted, "And kiss her vampiric ass."

A murmur of outrage rose from the crowd, but none moved. All continued watching the balcony.

Finally its two doors opened, and out stepped a man. He did not wear a general's uniform, but was dressed as a Norse god from myth. He was wrapped in a thick fur coat, and carried a giant hammer over one shoulder. His face was marked by scars that crisscrossed most of his visible skin, and one eye was completely white.

His full head of snowy hair flew out behind him as if he had just been struck by lightning, and it gave him a ferocious look when paired with his scars and deep features.

"A vampire in our midst, is it?" General Barskall asked with a sniff. "And not one of you all has brought me her head?"

Valerie laughed, loud and long. "You forgot the Goddess part. And some of your boys tried. You can ask them about it, or give it a go yourself and see what happens."

Anger flashed in his good eye, and he adjusted the war hammer so that he now held its handle with both hands.

"I'll tell you what," he declared. "First to bring me her tongue will be my right-hand man. I want to wipe my ass with it. Attached? Up to you."

"You've got a sick imagination," Valerie shot back before anyone could respond. "How's this for a counteroffer? Everyone here reject this man as your leader, then lay down your arms and get the hell out of here, never to cause trouble again. No threats from me. No childish demands." She turned to the crowd, getting real now. "And let me be clear. I do not believe I am a goddess, but I know for a fact anyone who stands in my way here tonight won't live to see the sun rise, so make up your minds."

Because she didn't want to kill anyone she didn't have to, she *pushed* an extra amount of fear as she drew her sword. The red of her eyes was reflected in its blade, and she smiled.

The silence that followed seemed to last forever, and was only interrupted by the sound of several dozen Weres retreating.

"Motherfuckers!" Barskall shouted, glaring at her. "You think you can come into my land and disrupt it like this? I'll have you know that I am a god. This isn't a pretense; this is simply me speaking the truth. You come in here saying you're a goddess? Well then, fucking own it—be the goddess you claim to be. Matter of fact, I'll take you into my godly bed right now and we can create little mini-gods, set up a whole kingdom. Doesn't that sound grand?"

She scoffed. "I'd rather parade you through the local cities on a leash like the dog you are while you beg forgiveness. How many people have you killed in this quest to feed your ego and prove to yourself that you are some amazing god?"

"People's lives are what you care about?" He spat. "They are nothing to us."

That was both what she had wanted him to say to condemn himself, and what she hated to hear. "You disgust me."

"So that's a no to the bedding, then?"

Leering, she shook her head. "That's a big fat *no*. And this is a middle finger, in case you can't see very well with the one eye." She held up her middle finger to add to the insult.

His good eye narrowed and his mouth moved as he searched for words, but finally he just shouted, "Kill her already!"

Chaos erupted with those words. More ran for their lives while others turned on Valerie. Those who had been following her were now stuck in the middle, but eventually ran—all but Berg, who fought at her side, she was pleased to see.

In that instant she removed her fur coat, tossing it to the side to land on an old cannon, and hefted her sword, ready for business.

Her goal was to separate the serious ones from those who

weren't, and that goal had been accomplished. Everyone remaining here would be dead soon, and she imagined the others would be too afraid of her return to cause real trouble any time soon.

She was a tornado, spinning and taking down Weres left and right, but after a few moments of this she saw Barskall turn as if to simply retreat to his chambers and be done with it. No way was that going to happen.

With a shout, she snatched a pistol from one of the Weres, cut off his arm and then his head, and threw the pistol at Barskall. It hit him upside the head so hard that it sent him sprawling, war hammer slamming into the floor in front of him.

He grabbed the hammer and leaped with a growl, landing with a thud a few feet from Valerie.

That war hammer missed her by inches as he swung, and it shattered the cement at her feet. She moved in to attack, and faster than she had expected, the war hammer came back at her. This guy wasn't a god, but he was damn fast and strong.

She leaped back, keenly aware that the Weres behind her were preparing to attack as well. As soon as she landed, she rolled sideways and came up charging.

Barskall parried attack after attack, but Valerie was done playing games. She might not be a goddess, but she was anointed by Michael himself—the Dark Messiah. She had no intention of letting this Were leave this place alive.

As the war hammer came at her again, she smiled, darted to her right, and cleaved one of his arms clean off. The momentum of the war hammer continued to propel both the weapon and his arm into the surrounding crowd.

His eyes burned with fury and hatred, and there was froth at his mouth. Now she got why he wasn't showing pain—he was on the drug. He turned to charge her, and transformed mid-step. She crouched, ready for a wolf, but instead she got a giant bear. It lunged, mouth wide open and trying to get her, but a sidestep and kick combined with the fact that it had only one front leg sent it to the ground at an odd angle. The bear twitched as his body tried to give out. While he wasn't likely feeling pain, fear sure was starting to show on his face.

Changing back, he leaped up and screamed, "Defend your god!"

She half-expected the Weres to laugh at him or retreat. They had seen him humbled; they had seen his weak side. However, to his credit he had apparently built himself quite the following.

Weres charged from all directions, transforming into their wolf forms as they ran. A group of large ones with shaved heads had grabbed Barskall and were helping him run, the coward!

Here she was, cleaving these sons of bitches in half while their leader fled.

She hacked at one, turned to kick another and, without letting her foot touch the ground, mule-kicked one behind her. There were so many though, that even with her speed, she was being overwhelmed. Not physically, but mentally—she didn't know where to attack.

A realization hit her—if there were so many that she didn't know where to attack, she could attack *anywhere* and hit her mark.

Now, instead of trying to hit them, she fell back into one of the old martial patterns she had practiced over and over in France. The sword swept around her, kicks and punches following; she was a tornado of steel that sent Were blood and body parts flying in all directions.

They couldn't touch her.

A *click* sounded, then she noticed movement on the general's balcony.

She couldn't stop moving—she was in the zone—but a sense of danger came over her as she felt new confidence in the air, coming from the Weres farther away.

Even as the Weres in the courtyard attacked, the ones on the balcony opened fire. Bullets tore through her flesh, and they took down the Weres around her too. Soon her attackers had backed off, but the shots kept coming.

Valerie felt her body convulsing, her lungs tearing open, other body parts giving out.

*FUCK!*

She rolled aside, piling Were bodies on top of herself to block the assault, pulling on more and more as she struggled to breathe with the collapsed lung and the blood pouring out of the wound in her throat.

Anger flared and she gave a hoarse, blood-gargling shout. Pain shot through her in new ways as her body pushed out bullets and arteries and tissue worked to knit themselves together. Had she been the old Valerie, before Michael had given her extra power, she would have been a goner.

As it was, this was the closest to death she had been since that day long ago when Donovan's men had left her to die. That was the day she'd decided to leave France behind, to stand up and fight for justice.

This was going to be a similar day, she realized. A day when she remembered how much she really hated pain. She was going to teach all these bastards a lesson. From this day forward, she was going to do everything possible, even more than she had been doing so far, to ensure that the world was safe, that pain would be at a minimum for the population of Earth going forward.

If there was an alien force out there, planning a war that would bring trouble? She was damn sure going to do her best to fight it.

While going into space had been a bit of a question in her mind before, she was now committed. But first, she had to deal with assholes like this Barskall piece of shit.

A full breath of air told her the lung was healed.

Pushing the dead Weres aside, she leaped up just in time to

see them mounting a Saw machine gun on one side of the balcony, a .50 cal on the other.

The words "Oh, shit" actually left her mouth without her having thought them first, and then she was diving as a fresh barrage of bullets came at her. It was almost too late when she realized these guys likely knew what they were doing, and were using the machine gun to lead her where they wanted her to be. She sprang sideways, pushing Weres out of her way and then...

*BOOM!*

The .50 cal had spoken, and Were body parts flew everywhere.

Weres were shouting, caught totally off-guard by this new tactic of not caring who was killed in this mad assault on her. They too were scrambling now to escape the courtyard, and Valerie ducked in with a group of them, then sprang onto the closest pillar and used it to push off, kicked against the side of the building, and leveraged her momentum to jump up to the balcony.

The two Weres manning the .50 cal saw her too late, and she sliced one's head off before cleaving the other at the legs. As he fell, she stood and jammed her blade between his eyes with a crunch.

The Weres with the Saw were trying to turn it on her, but she was faster and damn strong. She picked up the .50 cal, smiled wickedly, and pulled the trigger.

*BOOM!*

The kickback was intense, but nothing she couldn't handle. Two Weres were blasted from the balcony, while another who had been running took her second shot in the head. His corpse collapsed over the side of the balcony to land below with a thud, the bloody mess that was his head following shortly thereafter.

She could get used to this.

A quick glance showed her Berg just outside of the courtyard, struggling with two Weres.

"Berg, get back!" she shouted.

He didn't think twice before doing as told, and she let loose with a series of shots that left the two dead and several large holes in the wall nearby, one a little too close to Berg's head for his personal comfort.

"*Careful!*" he shouted, then added, "Please."

"Sorry!"

She spun, putting her sword into its sheath and grabbing the Saw as well, then unleashed both it and the .50 cal on the other side of the courtyard where several Weres were starting to climb the stairs that wound around the courtyard and would bring them to her.

Both the Weres and the stairs were obliterated.

"Where's Barskall?" she shouted, and Berg's head moved, searching.

"He went that way!" he replied, pointing.

If the guy was lying to her, he'd get his. But she had a feeling that, based on what he had just gone through for her, they were well beyond that point.

Machine guns at the ready, she leaped down, turned, and was off in pursuit. Other Weres appeared, a couple with rifles from upper windows of barracks, some on an old fort with a bit of a bunker to it. She ran through them all, blasting them with the two humongous guns as she went.

*At this point, it is just sad,* she thought.

While she was growing up she had learned about all the old religions, about a man who had come down from a mountain with tablets full of commandments or something like that and destroyed the false idols the people were worshiping. The story never made much sense to her, but running through this place killing these self-anointed gods left and right, she started to feel as that man might have felt. While she wasn't here to deliver ten commandments or anything like that, and really had no idea if there was any sort of God out there, she was certainly enforcing her own three commandments:

No more terrorizing the innocent.

No more injustice.

Never fuck with Valerie, Michael's Justice Enforcer.

The punishment was clear—complete and utter destruction.

At the end of the walkway between the now bullet-ridden buildings, she emerged into a field of old cannons and tanks, and saw the three bald men and Barskall climbing into an airship at the far end.

"You gotta be kidding me!" she shouted. How many damn airships did these people have? Well, she supposed she had only seen four now, but still, it was pissing her off. The pirates must have made off with antigrav technology, or done a good job of stealing airships from those who had.

She lifted both guns in front of her and shot as she ran, but halfway there a movement alarmed her. The tanks weren't mobile, but two were aiming at her.

A heavy sigh left her lungs just before the first shot went off. She threw herself backward so that it hit the building behind, causing part of it to crumble. These buildings were old, and a shot like that could do some real damage.

The .50 cal had fallen from her hands in the leap for safety, but she still had the Saw. She didn't think it would do much good against tanks, though, so she tossed it as the next shot came.

She imagined it would be a hard one to recover from if it hit her, so she threw everything into a leap forward, tucking as the shell flew by inches from her face. She landed with a roll as it exploded behind her.

No more playing around.

By the time the tank adjusted its aim, she had already closed the distance and leaped to the top of it. She pulled off the hatch and jumped in, and the Were inside turned and screamed at the sight of her with her red eyes glowing, *pushing* fear like crazy.

There wasn't room for glory and show here, so she simply snapped his neck and tossed him out of the tank. Closing the hatch, she looked at the controls, debating...then decided that it was probably too big of a pain. Too bad, because it would've been great.

Instead she turned, about to jump out of the tank and move on, when she spotted several rifles and a grenade launcher with three grenades attached on the far wall.

*Oh, this was going to be fun.*

She snatched the grenade launcher and jumped out, leaping aside as the other tank lobbed a shell at her. Before it had even hit, she ran over and pulled the other tank's hatch right off, tearing the metal. She smiled at the guy as he looked up in terror, threw a grenade into her launcher, and aimed.

"Should've run when I gave you the chance," she told him, and jumped back and into the air as she pulled the trigger.

The grenade found its mark, and the explosion rocked the tank. Smoke came out of the open hatch, and she gave it one last look as she took a moment to be impressed with herself before turning back to her objective.

Damn, the airship was already airborne.

She reloaded the launcher and aimed, then shot. The first grenade missed, exploding at the base of a tree downfield and splitting it up the middle.

The second grenade, however, hit the rear of the airship and left a big hole where the captain's quarters would normally be. The ship tilted but recovered, still moving forward. A gust of wind blew Valerie's hair across her face, carrying with it the scent of death and explosions. *What a smell*, she thought as she eyed her target.

Valerie dashed after the airship, eyes searching for any way to give chase, and then she saw that, during the explosion, one of the ropes connecting the ship to the balloon had been cut and was hanging down. Her eyes moved to the building to her right, noting the trajectory of the ship in relation to the building, and then to the light post next to the building and the tank at its base.

Her legs moved by instinct, and she dropped the grenade launcher to hold her sword in place as she ran. She jumped onto the tank, leaped onto the light post, and shinnied her way up.

The airship was moving fast, and was almost at the building.

She reached the top of the light post and pushed herself into a crouch, then threw herself at the building. The closest window had bars and a ledge. She grabbed those bars, used the ledge to brace her feet for leverage, and thrust herself upward to grab the edge of the roof. As she pulled herself up and over, she saw the airship passing, out of reach.

But the rope was still hanging, and it was not out of reach —she hoped.

She had no idea how she would find that prick up there if she didn't catch the rope, so she gave it her best shot. Running across the roof, she sprang off the far side, arms and legs flailing as she reached for the rope. She was falling...but her hand caught the rope at the last second and she held firm, refusing to let go even as she slid to its end and the friction tore away her skin.

With the arm that gripped the rope still weak from the earlier bullet damage even though she had mostly healed, she pulled herself up until her other hand was able to grab the rope. She scaled it hand over hand until she could wrap her legs around it and clench the rope with her feet. This action gave her a moment's respite, and she was able to catch her breath.

Everything that had just happened ran through her mind, and she started to laugh. Here she was, dangling from the rope of an airship that was quickly leaving behind the insane amounts of destruction she had just caused, and all she could do was laugh.

It was absurd and she knew it, but she couldn't help herself. The ridiculousness of it all combined with just how fun it had been, in a disturbingly weird sort of way. *Damn*, she was looking forward to killing this son of a bitch.

The airship had left the Den of the Gods far behind by the time Valerie finally shinnied up to the level of the now-exposed captain's quarters. Instead of going in that way, though, she pulled herself along the side of the ship with her claws and entered through a porthole that led to the main cabin, where sailors would sleep when they were on board, and where she figured she could hide.

While she wanted to just go in there and kill the bastards, she realized she needed to know where the ship was going. It only hit her as she was climbing that Berg was likely a low-level Were in this organization, and while he knew where the Den of the Gods as he had called it, was, Barskall might have another location, a hideout of sorts.

She laid low in the dark, watching the moon as they passed, listening for any sign that the Weres had found out she was aboard. Lucky for her—or for them, depending on how one looked at it—they were apparently up top, and the wind carried away any scent they might otherwise have picked up.

What this meant for finding Cammie and the others, Valerie wasn't sure. It wouldn't be easy to meet back up after this, at least not right away. That thought worried Valerie, giving her a sense of loneliness, of being cut off from the world, but she was better than that—bigger than that, really.

It wasn't her role in this life to be the needy one, the one who had to be with her friends at all times. Her job was to deal with evildoers like this prick Barskall, and that's what she was going to do.

As the night wore on she found herself leaning back in the darkness, closing her eyes, and getting some rest.

Her mind carried her off to dreams of New York, of Sandra waddling around with her belly protruding, and of placing her hand on that belly and feeling the baby kick. It was a pleasant dream, later interrupted by an image of Robin, in a Toronto that was being rebuilt, staring at the moon and thinking of Valerie.

When Valerie woke to feel the ship descending, she saw the moon lower in the sky now, approaching the horizon. The thought that Robin might be staring at that same moon on the other side of the ocean made her smile.

She stretched, cracked her neck back and forth since she had been sleeping in an awkward position, and then stood, preparing for the next phase in Operation Take Down Barskall.

# CHAPTER SEVENTEEN

## Among Giants

Not wanting to be found on board, Valerie went back to one of the airship's portholes and climbed out, noting that the ground was less than twenty feet below. She was preparing to jump when she saw what was no doubt their destination.

Rising from the ground ahead of them, silhouetted against the clear night sky, were the shapes of large Viking swords, as if they had been stuck into the ground by giants. These had to be some monument from the days before the Great Collapse, unless giants too existed in this world of vampires and Weres. She doubted it.

She stared in awe, then realized the ground was coming up fast. She even saw the forms of people moving ahead, among the monuments.

Without another moment's hesitation, she released her grip on the ship and rolled as she hit the ground, careful to hold her sword close so it wouldn't cut her or snag on something.

The airship came in low, forcing her to duck to avoid hitting her head as she came to a stop. It landed at the edge of a clearing, with the sword monuments just on the other side.

A glance around revealed the ocean on one side, which

explained the distant roar she could now hear, and trees and hills on the other. Looking toward the horizon provided another reason to stare in awe—the sky was glowing an almost turquoise green, unlike anything she had ever seen before.

Between the giant swords and this beautiful sky, she came close to understanding how one could feel a connection to the gods.

Someone ahead shouted, and she quickly picked herself up and darted partway around the clearing to approach from a different direction.

She recognized Barskall's voice shouting orders, though the language sounded slightly different then Norwegian. Valerie imagined it was Icelandic, meaning he was now among his true followers. Maybe a group of them had settled here with bigger plans to reach out into the world, expand their domain. Or maybe it was some form of worship for the ones who had come before, in some twisted way.

Tree branches brushed her as she snuck forward. When she reached the edge of the shadows, she saw that the green sky was casting its glow across a field of grass between the swords. Barskall and his three largest Weres, along with several others, had gathered in the field.

Many of them were shouting now, but Barskall stepped forward, raising the stump of the arm that had apparently healed enough to not be bleeding or nasty anymore, and shouted a string of words. One of them was easily understood. *War.*

Valerie had a feeling that would involve more people being hurt, as 'war' wouldn't simply refer to her.

A woman stood there gesturing at the ocean, and Valerie's best guess was that they were discussing whether to get their homeland and Barskall's family involved in some way. He was shaking his head.

Of course, these were only guesses.

He lifted his good arm, and one of them offered him a sword.

He pointed north with the blade, and the others gave a roar of approval, pulling out swords and guns.

This had gone on long enough.

Valerie drew her sword and moved along the outer edge of the clearing to where a couple of stragglers stood with their backs to her. With vampiric speed she dragged one back, covering his mouth as she thrust the sword into his chest, pulling him into the shadows. When he stopped moving she chopped off his head, held it by the hair, and lobbed it up and over the others so it hit Barskall in the chest with a *thump*.

She moved quickly so that she wasn't in the direction it had come from, and saw them all gazing at the head at Barskall's feet in shocked silence.

One of them sniffed the air, then another, and without a word, everyone except Barskall and his three henchmen stripped and transformed into wolves.

In quick movements, Valerie moved through the trees, being sure to drag her hand across their bark, hoping that would leave her scent.

The wolves formed a semicircle looking out, ruffs raised on their necks, teeth bared.

It was working. They couldn't get a clear scent, so they weren't sure where she was. To them, it was probably like being faced with an army of vampires, but they all smelled like the same vampire.

"So you *are* out there," Barskall shouted, stepping up behind the wolves. "How very fucking brave of you. First you slaughter my innocent army of gods, now you come to Asgard itself and want to take us down? Come on, then! Show yourself! Let me introduce you to my dear friend, Hel."

The female werewolf growled and stepped forward, and they all started moving. The hunt had begun.

Except that while the wolves thought they were the ones hunting, Valerie knew it was quite the opposite.

If only her friends were here to see this! What a fun time it would be. She moved back and climbed a tree, waiting. When the first wolf passed under her she was on it in an instant, plunging her sword down just as it looked up to follow her scent.

It managed a yelp, but by the time two other werewolves had arrived, she was farther into the forest dealing with another one.

As soon as that was done, she circled back and picked off those two, one at a time.

The large female he'd called Hel leaped out of nowhere, and Valerie cursed herself for getting careless. Teeth sunk into her shoulder and Valerie tried to swing her sword, but the angle was wrong.

Knowing she would heal, she slammed Hel into the nearby tree, scraping her along its bark, then dropped the sword and kicked it against the tree so that when she brought the wolf down, half her hide was skinned off.

Hel let out a yelp and released Valerie's shoulder, and that's when Valerie struck. Three good kicks to the wolf's head and it exploded all over the tree. The arm would take a couple seconds to heal, so she picked up the sword in her other hand and turned to see one of the bald men charging her.

"I've got you," he shouted, and the shout became a roar as he transformed into a bear. His paw's swipe nearly knocked over the tree, but Valerie had ducked and come up behind it. Her left-handed sword strike wasn't as well aimed as her right would have been, so she cut his backside instead of plunging the blade into him as she had meant to do.

He roared and spun, connecting with a paw to send her flying back into the clearing.

She landed hard, but quickly sprang to her feet and recovered her sword.

"There you are, little kitty," Barskall said through gritted teeth, and now he and the two Weres at his side transformed into bears, though he still only had one arm.

The bears roared and came at her together. With so many of their wolf companions down, though, their confidence had been dealt a blow. Valerie used that against them, *pushing* fear and shouting her loudest warcry as she brandished her sword. Two of them hesitated, leaving the third exposed.

She rolled to her left, slicing through his legs so that he stumbled forward and made the earth tremble with his fall. As he tried to recover, she moved on to the next. He swiped at her with both paws at once, mouth open in a roar.

"You have horrible breath," she noted, then stabbed the sword up and into his throat. When he fell face first into the ground, dead, she sniffed the air. "Ah, much better."

The next one plowed into her, knocking the sword from her grip. His claws dug into her flesh, but she had claws too. Hers tore into his neck and eyes, growing long like knives, and soon he was nothing more than a twitching mass on top of her.

She had started to push out from under the dead bear when Barskall was suddenly there in human form, swinging her sword at her head.

"Shit!" she shouted, barely moving out of the way in time. The sword struck stone and cut off a chunk of her hair. Oh, now she was *pissed*. She kicked the bear off her and went at Barskall, claws ripping him to shreds even as he tried to step back and swing her sword.

A good strike to the wrist and he dropped the sword, but she caught it, spun and sliced, spilling his guts onto the rocky ground.

"Witness your god," Valerie said to the last of them, then stepped forward, sword raised. "I give you a man." The sword sliced through his skull, stopping when it was lodged in the ground beneath. "Actually, I give you...a corpse."

The final one transformed into a man upon seeing this so that he could shout his leader's name as the sword fell and Barskall's life ended. He knelt because of the strike Valerie had landed on his legs. With heavy breaths, he stared dumbfounded at his companions' corpses.

"This wasn't supposed to happen," he grunted. "We were gods. We were invincible."

"None of us are gods," she replied. "You could've fled. You know that, right?"

"We'd rather die with him," the Were said, motioning to the corpse of Barskall, and glaring at her.

As she raised her sword, he transformed into a bear and lowered his head, ready for it.

"Your will be done," she hissed through gritted teeth, and brought down the sword, separating head from body. It was over.

# CHAPTER EIGHTEEN

**Trondheim**

Sunrise came too early. Cammie glanced around the hall, sad to see that there was still no sign of Valerie.

But there hadn't been any sign of violence on the part of the gods, either.

"If I find out she's lost out there and we could be in the sky searching while we're down here relaxing, I'll kill myself."

"Which way, boss?" William asked.

Cammie glanced around to find Royland, only to remember that he had returned to the ship the night before. She vaguely remembered him saying something about that; to keep watch and so that he wouldn't have to figure out how to get back in daylight. She wanted to ask him, but even while she was thinking this thought, it hit her.

"We go to these so-called gods."

William scratched his head. "I've been asking around, and I'll be honest... I don't think we have the strength to take them down."

"Maybe not, but if Valerie is there and needs our help, we can give it. If she's not there yet, you can be sure she'll find her way to them at some point, and that's when we strike."

They said their farewells to those who were awake, then began the trek back to the ship. Before heading out, they had agreed to take only one and leave the other ship for the people of Trondheim.

It wasn't long before they were airborne, William helming the ship so Reems could get some rest. He had insisted on standing watch for most of the night, since he was apparently much less of a party animal than William.

Cammie found Royland in bed, and she sat next to him, watching him sleep. It amused her, how powerful this man was, how scary he could be to his enemies—and how much he reminded her of a cute little kitten, the way he curled up and let out an almost purring sound in his sleep.

When she stood to go, his eyelids twitched, then slowly opened.

"Hey there," he said, reaching out to take her hand and pull her back down next to him. "Couldn't be without me?"

"More like I needed a booty call." She winked. When he raised an eyebrow and started to get up, she held out a hand, laughing. "Only joking. As much as I'd love it, you need your rest and we're just setting off. They'll need my eyes up there, and I have to be ready in case we face trouble."

"Ah, you don't want me wearing you out then," he said, lying back down with a sleepy grin.

"Exactly." She held his hand, rubbing it with both of hers. "You know...I've been thinking."

"Hmmm?" His eyelids grew heavy, but he was still listening, she knew.

"Maybe when we get back, we go find ourselves a dog."

"They don't exactly have dogs for sale at the local market," he replied with a laugh. "Where are we going to find one?"

She shrugged. "There was more than one out there the day we

found Elroy. I'd want a big one. Big and mean, so that it scares off anyone that might want to cause trouble."

"Wait, if we have that, what do I need you for?"

She hit him playfully. "You need me for a damn lot, Mister. Or maybe I disappear and we see how you survive without me."

"I'd be lost," he admitted. "And very emotionally and somewhat sexually deprived."

"Wow, I'm not sure if I'm supposed to be happy you put your emotional fix above your sexual one. I mean, I've been known to—"

"Hey now," he lifted his head, going up on one elbow, "I don't want to hear or think about what you've been known to do. Trust me, you more than astound me in every way, *especially* that way."

"Yeah, well, don't forget it." She stared into his eyes and asked, "So…"

"If you want a dog, of course we're getting a damn dog." His smile widened, and she could tell he loved the idea as much as she did.

Happy with the outcome of that conversation, she left Royland to sleep. Without Kristof and Elroy to keep her company, she would need the companionship of the dog, or have to figure out how to start sleeping in the day and staying awake at night. Maybe that could work out, too, once they got back. If the world was finally moving toward peace—or at least her section of it—she didn't see why it wouldn't.

Cammie made her way around the ship, checking on everyone and keeping watch for their destination. More trees and hills, and the clear fresh air she would miss like hell when they finally left this land.

Birds took off from an area south of them and at first Cammie thought it was nothing, but then she noticed movement below the trees—barely noticeable, like people wearing black or camouflage.

"What's that?" she said, pointing to movement in the distance.

The sailor next to her just shook his head, unable to see it. Her Were eyes gave her that extra bit needed though, and she squinted to get a good visual.

"There's a group of people on the move down there."

"Is Trondheim at risk?"

She went to the other side of the ship and looked back, trying to calculate the direction from which they'd come and project it against the direction in which the group seemed to be headed.

With a shake of her head, she turned back to the sailor. "I think they're clear."

He frowned, looking ahead and then back in the direction of the group, even though he still couldn't see them.

"You're thinking about something," she stated. "What is it?"

"If Valerie is fighting the gods, it might not be good to divert from our path at this point," he replied.

"Agreed. We've waited long enough." She stared out at the land, hands on the railing of the ship. It bothered her that there was a group moving around like that, but they really didn't look like they were going in any direction that would matter to her people.

They couldn't afford to stop and question every group they came across, after all.

Another half-hour of flying and they saw it—the military compound that she was sure was the place they were looking for. Her guess was confirmed by the smoke rising into the sky, fresh fires burning merrily in several places.

"What happened there?" Reems said, having asked one of his men to wake him when they spotted the facility.

"Valerie happened, I'm guessing," Cammie replied. "Which means we're probably too late. Take us over. Let's see what we can spot."

Others came on deck to get a look as they passed. The central courtyard was full of bodies, mostly Were, and most of the buildings were riddled with bullet holes or had been demolished by

164

explosions. They kept going and saw tanks, one with smoke still coming out of the opening on top, and a nearby building partially in ruins.

There was a launching ground where maybe an airship or two had been, but none were there now.

"She's gone," Cammie stated, certain of it.

"What now?" Reems asked.

"It's possible she'll linger once it's finished."

"If she succeeds, you mean," Reems interjected.

Cammie scoffed. "She always does. She always will. Yes, *when* she succeeds, she'll maybe look for us, but she'll eventually head west. We should follow that group we saw, whom I'm now guessing were the survivors of this fight. See where they go, then..."

She didn't want to say it, so she was glad Reems voiced the thought instead.

"We head back," he said.

"The chances of us coming across her here are slim. More likely we'll reunite with her when she returns."

"I'll tell William." Reems turned to convey the message, leaving Cammie to stare at the destruction and wonder where Valerie might have gotten off to. The woman could certainly handle herself, but that didn't make Cammie like it any better.

After a few minutes of this, the airship began to make the turn to go back. When it was straight and on a direct path west, Reems and William came out to brief the sailors.

"Ladies and gentlemen," Reems announced, pausing for dramatic effect, "we're going home!"

The sailors cheered, likely glad to not have gotten involved with the kind of death and destruction they had just seen below.

Cammie wasn't exactly sure how to feel, but found herself smiling along with the rest of them. She wished it had gone differently, that she could have stayed with Valerie, but now she was certain Valerie was taking care of the bandit problem, while they had brought Kristof home and helped solve his city's problems. With the gods' base destroyed, they likely wouldn't mete out any sort of retribution on Trondheim.

Oddly, a part of her was relieved that she hadn't spilled more blood on this trip. It was a weird feeling, because she tended to get a high from the fighting. She had always enjoyed it, even looked forward to it to a degree. Now she was happy to have kept it to a minimum; she wondered what was happening to her.

In fact, she was happy to be going home, and looked forward to spending some downtime with Royland.

## CHAPTER NINETEEN

**Meldal**

It was tough flying the airship by herself and making her way north, but by midday she had located Meldal and touched down. She was met by Hans, who told her that nobody named Cammie had come through, but she had others waiting for her. As he led her to the city center, he glanced at the damaged airship she had arrived in.

"You might do better with a smaller ship, and we're in need of a larger one," Hans said. "Perhaps a trade is in order?"

"You have something smaller?"

He held up a hand, then simply beckoned her to follow him. When they turned the corner into a small grassy area next to a garden, she saw why he was smiling. It was a single-passenger airship, just big enough for her to fly and, he claimed, with controls easy enough not to confuse her.

"Thank you! This will be perfect." She turned back to the city center. "Berg?"

He nodded. "I don't know what you did to that man—to any of them, really—but they've changed."

"After what I've been through?" She laughed. "I'd fucking hope so."

"Maybe we can learn to live in peace after all," he said. "Do what you must here, and I'll ready the airship for your departure."

He pointed her to where she would find many of the Weres who had fled, with Berg at their center. He had been telling them what was going to happen now, giving them orders, but he paused at the sight of Valerie.

All remaining Weres transformed and bent down, front legs out, and bowed their wolf heads.

*This wasn't the first time something like this had happened*, she thought, remembering the Golden City Weres.

Many of those had turned out to be treacherous, she had learned when speaking with Sandra.

She wasn't about to make that mistake again.

"Go home," she said. "Never use your Were ability again, and especially not for wrongdoing, or I will come after you." She walked over to the wolf she was sure was Berg, and gestured to him. "Berg will lead those of you who wish to accompany him back to Iceland, where you will start a new community. Those of you who stay here must watch yourselves. Keep your eye on every dark alley, and pray to some real god—not yourself—that I don't have a reason to come back. Because if I do, there will be hell to pay."

With that the rest of them broke, many sauntering off, confused that their reign of terror had finally come to an end.

Berg, however, didn't seem to know what to think. He had transformed as she finished speaking and now stepped forward, arms out, to present her with the fur coat she had left at the military compound.

"Didn't want you to get cold, so I went back for it."

She smiled, shaking her head. "If you got blood on it, you're finding me a replacement." Putting it on, she turned for him to inspect it. As far as she could tell, there was no blood. Now, *that* was miraculous. Maybe there were gods around here after all.

"It's perfect," he admitted after watching her spin a couple times to confirm it. "I just can't believe you pulled it off. I mean, you terrified *me*, but that man... The things he's done. He has given me nightmares since I met him. Shit, I might actually sleep soundly for the first time in years, if I don't dream of you now."

"Now you'll have nightmares of me?"

"I didn't say..." He blushed. "Point is, wow. Just...*wow*."

"You do right, got it?" She ignored his dreaming comment, glancing around to get her bearings. "You know I won't hesitate to kick your butt, and one of my kicks will send you into the ocean."

"I believe you."

"Good." She considered him, then a thought hit her. "At the military compound, I saw riches. Treasure. I'd bet that could do a lot of good if distributed around to the various communities, maybe used in setting up trade with others around Europe, maybe New York."

"Thank you," he said. "You can count on me."

"I know I can, because if you mess it up, you know I'll be back with a vengeance."

He chuckled, then waved as she headed for the small airship and Hans.

She paused momentarily, hearing Berg giving orders to those who had decided to go with him, and smiled.

He might have been one of them, but in his heart, he wasn't really. She saw that in his eyes, too, and if there was one thing she prided herself on, it was knowing whom to trust. Of course, the fact that she could almost read minds, in the form of sensing emotions, might have had something to do with it.

Now it was time to return to her friends and see if they had reunited the boy with his family. If that was done, she was looking forward to getting out of this place. It didn't have Cammie, or Sandra, or the others. It didn't have Robin...

Sunrise hit the surrounding hills, casting a pink hue over the land that made her pause in appreciation.

But as beautiful as it was, it simply wasn't home—wherever the hell home was.

Hans was at the airship, and had her all ready to go. He offered supplies and payment, but she refused, except for a few of their Norwegian pastries—they just looked too damn good to pass up.

After a nod of appreciation, he stared at her, concern and awe showing in his expression. "You know where you're going?"

"I suppose I'll try Trondheim, see if my friends are there."

"And if they aren't?"

"I don't even know where to start."

"If it was me, and knowing you?" He laughed, holding his belly. "I'd believe you could handle yourself, and probably assume you would make it back to the American continent."

"You think so?"

He shrugged. "I don't know for certain, but I'll tell you one thing. You sure as hell aren't going to find your people by flying randomly around here. The skies are too vast. The ground, well, there's just too much of it to cover and not miss each other."

She nodded, hating that he was probably right. If he was, she figured it made sense to try for a bit, but then what? Head back immediately? No, she wasn't quite ready for that.

The trip to Trondheim was painless, the journey in the small airship relaxing. It had been a long night and morning, and even with the extra energy Michael's powers bestowed upon her, she still needed rest from time to time.

She had seen the city on the way over, and worked her way to the coast. She put the ship down on a hill nearby, and walked the rest of the way.

Soon she was passing through a residential neighborhood.

Judging by the few islands out in the water and way the waves broke past them, this area too had experienced some flooding at some point in its relatively recent history. She spent the day exploring the town, keeping a lookout and staying to the shadows, but by the time evening approached she'd figured out that they weren't here. Maybe they would be back, if they had already been through, or maybe they had been out looking for her and hadn't arrived yet.

As much as she wanted to get on with this journey, she had to admit to herself that it could wait until morning. Her best bet was to find a rooftop, lean against a chimney, and get some shuteye, so that's exactly what she did.

A dream came in the night, of her, before she had set off for America, back when she had to hide from the daylight to avoid dying. When the rays of light hit her in the morning, she woke with a start and drew back, almost believing the sun would burn her alive.

No such thing happened, to her relief, and then she remembered where she was. She picked herself up and began walking through the city again, unsure where to start. Some men and women sold grilled meat on sticks, others hats and different garments they had made, and she had to smile at the idea of this city thriving here despite what she had seen in the last two places she had visited.

It was even more amazing considering they didn't know what had happened with the Weres yet. They didn't know they were free, and yet they went about their lives as best they could.

She stopped to ask one old lady about an airship, but the woman stared at her, then shrugged and walked away.

The next group did the same, but when she asked a lady about Kristof and showed her how tall he was by holding her hand at about the height of her ribs, the lady's face lit up and she pointed.

"I show you," the lady mumbled as she grabbed Valerie's hand and pulled her along.

It was an odd feeling, being dragged through the streets by this very normal lady. Valerie liked it, thinking that it made her feel more human again. More like one of them.

"There," the woman said, then pointed to the sky and said something in Norwegian."

"Sorry, I…"

"Early," the woman said, and pointed to the location of the sun, still close to the horizon.

Valerie nodded, getting it. She thanked the lady, then waited a bit, sitting on the steps opposite the house. When she saw movement in a window, she bolted up and knocked on the door.

A lady with curly blond hair opened the door and frowned.

"Kristof?" Valerie asked.

Again the lady frowned, but this time there was a shout from behind her in Norwegian and the boy appeared.

"Valerie," he said, eyes wide in shock. "They… They're gone."

That hit her hard. She had very much expected to find them here. Without them she didn't have a ship to get back in, though she could call Sandra with the comm device and probably find someone to come get her. And there was always the idea of swimming back across the ocean, but she doubted it was realistic.

"Do you know where they went?"

Kristof frowned, but nodded. "Sorry, but in all the confusion I didn't hear where they would go first."

"Thank you." Valerie smiled, tamping down her frustration. She turned to go, then glanced back. "You know, I almost forgot to congratulate you. It must feel nice to be back with your family."

He nodded as his mom appeared behind him and wrapped her arms around him.

"It does," he replied, then waved goodbye as she left.

*Family*, she thought, wondering how that term applied to her now. She was on her own, and it was time to accept that. At least, until she returned to America.

# CHAPTER TWENTY

**New York**

While the city went about its evening routine, Sandra prepared a tray of lemon tarts—something she had been wanting to try out for the café for a while now. But it really wasn't about that, she had to admit to herself as she arranged them on the platter. It was about taking her mind off thoughts of Diego.

If he never came home, this baby would be born without a father. Her mind kept going to images of him getting shot out there, the Pod crashing and falling into some lake he couldn't escape from, even crazy thoughts like alien ships appearing from the sky and taking him away for testing. She was being paranoid, and she knew if she told anyone, that would be exactly what they would say.

She focused on the lemon tarts instead. But who was she kidding? The thoughts kept coming, regardless.

She resolved to get out of there and go for a walk. Since she didn't have anywhere she needed to be, she decided she would first head over to the wall and see how the rebuilding of the city's defense system was going. It wasn't perfect, but they wanted to be ready in case there was backlash. If any group didn't like what they were up to or detected their actions toward disabling the indie network, there might be attacks on the city.

They couldn't let that happen.

The sun had set and she wondered about the time difference where Valerie was, remembering how odd the timing had been on their flight from Europe the first time. She glanced at the comm device, which she always kept nearby now in case Valerie called. She wanted to call and ask her—or just hear her voice—but was sure that distracting her at the wrong moment would be disastrous. She would wait for Valerie to contact her instead.

Reaching the walls, she had to admire the work they had done. This was so much better than it had been when she had first arrived in this city. They had asked people to work after giving them first aid supplies, food, and more, and they were working hard for their city. They had been inspired to contribute.

If she could get this possible theater going, it might start to feel like a cohesive society. *Dream big or go home*, she told herself, examining the defenses again. The gates were reinforced steel, and the walls sported gun turrets and bore extra protective layers against attacks from both below and above. Above wouldn't happen anytime soon, but it was better to be prepared in case there was an enemy out there who came with surprises.

As she stood on the wall, she turned, squinting, and felt a pinch on her lip as she bit it. Without realizing it, she had let the excitement get to her—but saw that it had been earned. The shape quickly approaching was definitely a Pod, and the only logical assumption she could make was that it was Diego and the others returning.

*If he was hurt, she would find whoever had done it and kill them herself*, she thought for the thousandth time since he had left.

"Sorry, I gotta get back to HQ," she said with a nod to the guard.

She darted off, making her way back down the steps and

starting to run toward the tall building with its blue stripe up the side. She had taken only a few steps when a pain hit her stomach, so she had to stop and sit down, holding her belly.

"Do you need help?"

She looked up to see Jackson standing there with a smile on his face and a smear of lipstick on his cheek.

"Just catching my breath," she said, but couldn't help laughing. "I take it you had a good time." She touched her cheek, then pointed at his.

With a confused frown, he touched his cheek, then looked at the smear of lipstick on his fingers and joined her in laughter as he sat down at her side.

"I don't kiss and tell, but you can figure it out, apparently."

She looked at him, curious. "May I ask...do you ever miss Valerie?"

His brow furrowed, but then he smiled again. "Not as much as you do, I'll bet. Do I think about her? Sure. She was powerful and different. With her, I was the one who needed looking after. Both sides of that coin have value."

Sandra nodded, glancing up to see the Pod disappearing around the back of HQ.

"Diego?" Jackson asked.

She nodded.

"Ah, so this time you were the lonely one." He stood and offered her a hand, and she took it. "I'll help you get over there so you can get that lonely bug out of your system."

As they started walking, she nodded, lost in thought.

"What is it?" he asked.

"What you said. She is powerful, yeah. Definitely different. Strong-willed and, I don't know, as much as I loved you two being together because of the smile it brought to her face, I just never really felt it made sense for her to be with one person. It's like, she's bigger than relationships."

"She still has womanly needs," he argued with a chuckle.

"So she gets men to do her bidding and please her, or women." A thought of her kiss with Valerie long ago brought up that thought, and though Valerie wouldn't admit it, Sandra had always felt that the kiss had meant a great deal more to Valerie than she had let on.

"Our Val?" Jackson laughed. "Sure, maybe. You know, I studied old mythologies some, and there are quite a few of them where the gods were almost like you and me, just...more powerful. Back then, or in those made-up times, the gods didn't differentiate love or lust with men or women so much. Same with certain ancient groups of warriors."

"Well, count me out of all that." Sandra shook her head, considering a life without Diego, even pausing for a moment to remember the last time they had been intimate. It sent a shiver up her spine.

"To each their own, I say."

"I'd say cheers to that, if I could drink." She put a hand on her protruding belly and smiled. "Maybe cheers to that in a few months."

He shook his head. "Then you got breastfeeding, right?"

"Dammit, thanks for reminding me. Do you think they had some alternative to that back in the old days? I mean, before the Collapse. I'm always so curious."

"It's possible. They certainly lived a life of luxury in many ways back then."

She nodded, thinking back to the stories she had heard about the old days.

They had just reached HQ when Diego came running through the doors. He paused at the sight of her, and as he approached she saw that his face was riddled with guilt and worry.

"What trouble did you get us into this time?" she asked.

He shook his head, rubbed a hand through his hair, and shrugged. "We're going to have a bit of a problem on our hands pretty soon."

"Diego?" She took the last two steps and wrapped him in her arms, kissing him firmly. When she pulled back, she held his gaze. "Tell me what's going on."

He gave a big sigh and told her everything. All she could think was that it was about time to double-check their defenses, get the troops riled up, and probably use that comm device sooner rather than later. If they were going up against several communities, including possibly Weres and Forsaken, they could certainly use some help.

# CHAPTER TWENTY-ONE

**Old France**

Valerie flew the one-man—or in this case, one-woman—airship in the general direction of where she guessed her old home had been. It took a while, and a few changes in direction, but before long she was sailing along in the early sunrise and spotted an unmistakable sight—the Eiffel Tower, still on its side, as she'd last seen it.

Somehow she had expected it to be fixed by now. Not that it had been *that* long, but a part of her, the part that had held out hope for humanity here, had expected them to finally get off their asses and rebuild the symbol of national pride.

Instead, it laid there limply, a river pouring past it and into the cracks of the broken ground nearby. The people of Old Paris had simply abandoned this part of town.

It was a stark reminder of why she had never felt she totally fit in here. Well, there was the whole vampire aspect of her life that separated her from the rest of humanity, of course, but there had been quite a few vampires in Old Paris in her day. She hadn't fit in with non-modified humans, and she certainly hadn't fit in with the vampires.

She had since learned that being a vampire didn't mean you had to be evil. It didn't mean you had to be a dick, either, though none of the men in her life back then had made her think otherwise.

Now she had returned to her homeland, and it felt more foreign than ever.

*Why had she made this trip*, she asked herself for the hundredth time. Something inside had just yearned for it, she decided finally, especially after being separated from her friends for so long. She had to believe they were safe, had to believe that they would make their way back to New York or Prince Edward Island and that she would one day return to find them happy and well.

She still had the comm device. She picked it up, gazing at it. A couple of calls had come in from Sandra during the journey, but Valerie hadn't been ready to talk to her. She hadn't wanted to admit she was going back to France, because it seemed...weak. She shouldn't have felt so compelled to return, but she had.

A word that popped into her head: closure. That was a large part of it, she was sure.

*Closure.* She had to see this place one last time. Find out who she had been here, so she would know who she could be going forward. There would be no more ignoring her past, trying to pretend it didn't happen. It was part of her, and had helped her become the woman she was now.

As she flew past, she noticed a couple of early risers glancing up at her, intrigued. She smiled and pulled her head back inside so that all they saw was the small airship. Turning to the west, she allowed herself one last glance at the Eiffel Tower, remembering that long-ago kiss with Sandra as they had sat together sharing that same view.

How far she had come since then, and yet part of her was that same woman, although now she had a purpose. It wasn't to fit in, to explore herself or her sexuality, though she was sure there would be time for that at some point. Her purpose now was to be part of something bigger. She would do everything in her power to protect the people of Earth, and at that moment promised herself she would find a way to get into space to join that war.

Maybe that would be with TH and his followers, or maybe Michael would come back for her.

A thought hit her, and she pulled out the comm device again. What if Michael *had* returned, and that was why Sandra had been calling? What if Valerie had missed the call, and Michael was leaving without her?

She made for the old military compound, her last stop. She had to know if Michael had accomplished his goal and dealt with the Duke.

When she finally spotted it, a white-grey building hidden in the trees, she took the comm device and called Sandra.

"Tell me Michael hasn't returned," Valerie barked immediately.

Sandra paused, silent, then said, "What? No, but…Val?"

"What is it?"

"We might be in trouble here. We've put the word out to Colonel Walton to see if they have anyone who can help, but it would be great if you could make it back here too."

"For what? What's happened?"

"It's the final showdown. Every group of indies, all the local nomad tribes, bandits, Were clans, and even some Forsaken, have joined forces and called us out for one final battle."

"You must've pissed them off good," Valerie exclaimed, shaking her head. "But this could be the best thing. End it once and for all, right?"

"So you'll come?"

Valerie looked down at the military compound, seeing no sign off life, none of the early morning training she had been used to for most of her life. It looked vacant; totally abandoned. She didn't need to see more than that.

"Girl, I'm on my way."

Valerie adjusted her course. She had seen enough. When she first arrived she had thought about walking the streets of Paris, smelling its scents and remembering what it had been like, but now she found none of that mattered. Her closure came in the form of remembering that her friends needed her, and she damn sure wasn't about to let them down.

"Farewell," she said with a final glance at her home country. "*Au revoir.*"

# EPILOGUE

**<u>Toronto</u>**

Staring out into the night, Robin thought for the thousandth time that no matter how much she loved it here, her calling was elsewhere. She had to be part of something bigger. With her powers, and after experiencing the way Valerie devoted herself to making the world a better place, Robin knew that was her path as well.

Her parents were safe. She had seen to it, and now it was time to see that the rest of the world was safe too.

Hitching her pack onto her shoulder and checking that her assassin garb was fastened properly so she safely could venture into the sunlight, Robin stood in the doorway, contemplating leaving without saying good-bye. It would be easier that way, wouldn't it?

She had just turned to go when she heard someone clearing his throat.

"It's going to happen this way," her father began, stepping into the dim moonlight, which was coming into the room through the gaps in the blinds.

"Dad..."

"You want to fight to save the world? Fine, but then so will we."

She frowned, confused.

"Your mother and I have been talking, and we agree that this place holds too many negative memories for us." He cleared his throat again, then stepped forward and held his hand out for her pack. She gave it to him.

"So, what now?"

"We go with you to New York," he replied. "We bring guns and ammunition, the first shipment of many we'll oversee from New York, with people we trust managing this side of it here. We'll establish a system of trade to ensure that New York and Toronto stand as two beacons of freedom and security in this crazy world."

She blinked, unable to come up with any reason this wasn't a good idea.

"And if I don't stay in New York?" she asked.

"You do what you have to do, and you can leave knowing we're surrounded by people you know and, I hope, trust. You have to leave for some time? Fine, but at least you know where we'll be, and we'll know you have a place to come back to, with easy access."

They stood there for several moments, Robin's breath coming heavily, and then finally she ran forward, wrapping her arms around her dad in a tight embrace.

"So you agree?" he asked.

"I love it," she confirmed, and then sighed with relief. She had looked forward to going to New York, and couldn't be happier about her parents coming as well.

The one question nagging at the back of her mind was how she felt about Valerie being there.

She decided that was a topic to be dealt with when and if it came up.

For now, she had a road trip with her parents to prepare for.

# AUTHOR NOTES - JUSTIN SLOAN

WRITTEN AUGUST 29, 2017

This is the life, isn't it? I write books about characters I love, share them with readers I love, and then we all just sit back and enjoy life? Ha. If only it were that easy—but it can be, as long as we keep a positive mind. So much drama and B.S. is going on around us. I truly believe we just need to be kind to others and do what we can do to make the world a better place. So much of it is out of our control.

So, why stress?

I will continue to write books I love, and try to keep a positive style throughout, ALWAYS bringing you a happy ending (or at least what I consider a happy ending). I don't want to be the writer who depresses the hell out of you. If you want that, I have written one or two books that have moments that are dark (Land of Gods? Mohira—under a pen name), but you know what? They always go to an uplifting place and, I hope, will make you a happier person.

I have so many reasons to be happy with life right now! As you may know, I went to writing fulltime recently. That's why we've been able to bring you these extra books relatively quickly, and why I've been able to work on some other projects on the side. My Syndicate Wars series (more coordinated by me than written by me) has done quite well, and we're doing spinoffs on that like Michael Anderle has done in the KGU world. I have brought two collaborators to the Creative Writing Career podcast to chat about it—you can check that out and tell me what you think. I'm excited, because I've been reading their stories and they rock. Then there are my spinoffs and solo series, including one that has magic in space, and another that is more paranormal in space (there are dragons too, but don't tell anyone!).

And of course... OF COURSE there are amazing things coming down the KGU pipeline. As if you didn't have enough other books from all of these collaborators, there will be a scifi one coming soon (probably with PT Hylton), and before that Craig and I will release something that bridges that gap. I also still have two Age of Magic books to do, and a very amazing narrator is reading those audiobooks for us (Kate Rudd is sticking with these Reclaiming Honor books, so I wanted to get someone different for those ones, to differentiate the series).

So yes, I'm loving fulltime author life. I was pretty worried, because I sold a screenplay a while back and was supposed to do three rewrites on it. Now it's time, as they want to shoot soon, but if I had a job there would be no way I could fulfill the commitment. Thanks to you all and Michael and my ability to be fulltime, I can actually do those obligated rewrites without serious upheaval.

We've been talking about what to do if all of these books continue to sell as they have and (I hope) sell even more as my solo series come out, and one idea is we relocate to Carlsbad or Santa Monica—be a bit closer to Disneyland for the kids (Yeah, right! Of course it's for me), and closer to Los Angeles in case the screenwriting thing kicks off. Maybe get back to acting, too.

On that note...did you know I used to act? Yeah, when I was in the Marines I would go to auditions all the time, and even had some small roles. I was in the Lacy Peterson movie as a policeman, as well as a lot of shorts and things like that. Nothing big, but I was an extra on the Veronica Mars show for a bit, which was cool. And while doing that, the casting agent had me and a bunch of other actors pretend to be terrorists in a fake Afghan town, for Marines to come through and train. We would use paintball guns and ambush them, and they would put us in handcuffs and / or kill us with paintballs. Those were fun times! I only mention it because the other day one of my readers looked me up on IMDB and was like "Whoa, how come you never talk about that stuff!" So there you go, consider it talked about. That might be something I'd like to get back into at some point too. I can imagine it now, sitting at a café working on my next Michael Anderle collaboration, then running over to audition for my role in the next Michael Anderle film or HBO show —right? RIGHT?

*Let's make it happen!*

I'll work my angles if you keep working yours (yours, by the way, are to just do what you've been doing—reading the books, being awesome fans and friends, and helping us out with word of mouth and reviews).

I think we have the better end of that deal, but hey, if you want to write too, jump on in. It's a very fulfilling life and / or hobby. There's now a Facebook group for fan fiction in the Kurtherian Universe, if you want to join us there. It hasn't really gotten off the ground yet, but maybe you can help us out with that! https://www.facebook.com/groups/TKGFansWrite/

Thank you for sticking with me! Wow, can you believe we're about to move on to book eight already? It's been a really exciting journey, and we've seen some fun reviews along the way. Some of you did NOT like Valerie exploring herself. LOL. I mean, wow! In my mind, these characters have to be real people, not just robots or cutout dolls I can play with. Their emotions and everything they're dealing with have to be in the story. Maybe this is because that's what *I* enjoy reading? Also, probably because I enjoy writing it. If I'm not enjoying writing or reading my own work, you can bet it would be dry.

Plus, let's be honest—my books would be very short if there wasn't any of that stuff in them. I can only write an uppercut or teeth tearing out a throat so many ways. But I'll try to come up with new ones, I promise!

In the meantime, I would sincerely appreciate it if you would leave a review for this book on Amazon. Also, check out the Facebook page (Reclaiming Honor), and feel free to roam over to www.JustinSloanAuthor.com to see what else I am up to. Thanks!

First, THANK YOU for not only reading this book - but also sticking until the end and reading these author notes as well!

One more book. That's it.

One more book to wrap up Valerie's story before she meets that 'special someone' in Michael's life...But, unfortunately, you will have to wait until TKG21 for the unfolding of that story.

Sorry! (Yes, I HAVE read the reviews that were not pleased with Craig not sticking in more information. You will have to let me unveil that in the final book of Bethany Anne's first series. Can't be jumping the line now.

Right now, I'm typing this after a day of conference calls, meetings, etc. etc. and even though it has been a 12 hour day so far, (like Justin) I'm not complaining. This is the most fantastic opportunity *anywhere*.

For those wondering about Darkest Before the Dawn - The Second Dark Ages Book 03 (Michael's Return) I am co-authoring it with Ell Leigh Clarke and we are finishing the beats today (two of the calls) and tomorrow.

Then, "It's WRITING TIME!"

Yes, I totally was thinking of the THING from Fantastic Four when I typed that. Hell, I can still hear Ben Grimm's voice in my head.

I'm curious. How many of you visit Las Vegas? The reason I ask is I have a completely OFF THE WALL idea about creating a location near downtown where I could put a publishing ... workspace? That I and other authors would use, and also mention when we would be in town to meet with fans.

I realize it's a kooky idea. But, you know, I rather like it.

Come to Vegas, gamble your money, see the shows, visit LMBPN World headquarters of The Kurtherian Gambit and Oriceran Universes and get a t-shirt, right?

SNICKER! I just thought "And get a picture with a life-sized (but HEAVILY Photoshopped) cut-out of the Author while you are here!" Plus, when I am in town, I'd go hang there from time to time and work...And just meet people.

I *doubt* anything will come of the idea, but you know... We (the authors and you the fans) have done some pretty crazy stuff before so I wouldn't put it past us.

LMBPN Publishing (my company) is closing in on our best month ever, and all I can say is THANK YOU.

Without your support, and crazy reading abilities and talking us up, we can't do what we do, and I wouldn't be blessed to give back to these authors who are making it happen every damned week.

In September, we are planning TWELVE releases. That is a record for us and we are looking at a time when we will have to separate the calendars between the two Universes.

That time isn't now, but I imagine it will be here by the end of the year.

If you are in Europe during the Frankfurt Book Fair, let me know. I'd like to setup a small get together with you!

October 11th-15th 2017 (http://buchmesse.de/en/tickets/ )

*ESPECIALLY* if you live in Frankfurt, let me know!


Ad Aeternitatem,
Michael Anderle

BOOKS BY JUSTIN SLOAN

## SCIENCE FICTION

**RECLAIMING HONOR** (Vampires and Werewolves - Kurtherian Gambit Universe)

**Justice is Calling**

**Claimed by Honor**

**Judgment has Fallen**

**Angel of Reckoning**

**Born into Flames**

**Defending the Lost**

**Return of Victory**

Shadow Corps (Space Opera Fantasy - Seppukarian Universe)

**Shadow Corps**

**Shadow Worlds**

**Shadow Fleet**

War Wolves (Space Opera Fantasy - Seppukarian Universe)

**Bring the Thunder**

**Click Click Boom**

**Light Em Up**

Syndicate Wars (Space Marines and Time Travel - Seppukarian Universe)

**First Strike**

The Resistance

Fault Line

False Dawn

Empire Rising


FANTASY


The Hidden Magic Chronicles (Epic Fantasy - Kurtherian Gambit Universe)

Shades of Light

Shades of Dark

Shades of Glory

Shades of Justice


FALLS OF REDEMPTION (Epic Fantasy Series)

Land of Gods

Retribution Calls

Tears of Devotion


MODERN NECROMANCY (Supernatural Thriller)

Death Marked

Death Bound

Death Crowned


CURSED NIGHT (Supernatural Thriller with Werewolves and Vampires)

Hounds of God

Hounds of Light

Hounds of Blood (2018)

**ALLIE STROM** (MG Urban Fantasy Trilogy)

Allie Strom and the Ring of Solomon

Allie Strom and the Sword of the Spirit

Allie Strom and the Tenth Worthy

# BOOKS BY MICHAEL ANDERLE

For a complete list of books by Michael Anderle, please visit:

**www.lmbpn.com/ma-books/**

All LMBPN Audiobooks are Available at Audible.com and iTunes. For a complete list of audiobooks visit:

**www.lmbpn.com/audible**

# CONNECT WITH THE AUTHORS

**Justin Sloan Social**

**For a chance to see ALL of Justin's different Book Series
Check out his website below!**

**Website: http://JustinSloanAuthor.com**

**Email List: http://JustinSloanAuthor.com/Newsletter**

**Facebook Here:
https://www.facebook.com/JustinSloanAuthor**

**Michael Anderle Social**

**Website:
http://kurtherianbooks.com/**

**Email List:
http://kurtherianbooks.com/email-list/**

**Facebook Here:**
https://www.facebook.com/TheKurtherianGambitBooks/

www.ingramcontent.com/pod-product-compliance
Lightning Source LLC
Chambersburg PA
CBHW022022120726
47898CB00008BA/2526